THE BODYGUARD

THE KING FAMILY BOOK TWO

S. DOYLE

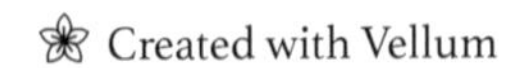
Created with Vellum

To Molly for making this happen. To Julie for leading us through. But most of all to our readers! We hope you enjoy this story as much as we did putting it together.

To find more of our stuff and great deals on the latest romance releases join the BBRL Book Club on Facebook or our Bad Boy Lovers Newsletter.

1

SABRINA

The King's Land—The Summer of Dylan

"Dylan. I want next. I want next!" I was hopping up and down with my hand in the air so he would see me.

He couldn't not see me. We were all out by the open horse pen. Bea and I were sitting together on the fence, while Dylan walked Ronnie around on the horse. Hank had taught him to ride.

Hank didn't think girls needed to ride horses so he didn't bother to teach us. But I wanted to ride. At least, I wanted Dylan to show me. He'd been here for weeks this summer, he was fourteen and he was the most fun.

"You're making such a big deal about him. He's just here for the summer," Bea snapped.

I looked over at my half sister. She was nine, only a year older than me, but she didn't like me too much. I knew it was because Hank married my mom right after her mom died. So she hated my mother, and she barely tolerated me. And that was sad because we could have been great sisters.

"He's our big brother," I pointed out. Which was the best thing in the world of things to have. Dylan let me follow him wherever he went. And he played with me sometimes, only not dolls. Today he was teaching us to ride a horse. It was totally scary, but I wanted to do it if he wanted to teach us.

"You don't even know him," Bea huffed.

"I do too!" I protested. Well, I knew he was Dylan and he was my big brother and he was nicer to me than Bea was. Hank had never married his mother at all, but he wasn't mean to Ronnie or Bea.

Bea shook her head in that way that she did that said she was so much smarter than me just because she was a year older.

"He's just a kid staying with us for the summer. You shouldn't get too close."

"But I like him. He's funny and he...pays attention to us."

Bea frowned. "Right. You shouldn't get too close to him. He's only going to disappoint you."

I watched as he helped Ronnie down from the horse and they high-fived. I didn't care what Bea said. I hopped off the fence and ran in his direction. I got to his side and tilted my head and looked back up at him with my goofy smile. At least, that's what Ronnie called it.

"My turn."

He shook his head and laughed. And then he had to pick me up to help me onto the horse, which was awesome. He grunted a little, but I didn't mind.

"Okay Brin," he said. "Hold the reins, but don't pull on them. We're just going to walk you once around the pen, okay? You need to just sit tight. Okay?"

"Okay, Dylan. Anything you say."

"Be careful with her, Dylan," Ronnie said, taking a few steps back and watching him closely.

"Don't worry. I won't get her hurt," he said.

Of course he wouldn't. He was my big brother. Big brothers never let you down.

SABRINA

The King's Land—Three Years Later
Hank's Summer Barbecue Blowout

"He loves me. He loves me not. He loves me. He loves me not. He loves me. He loves me not."

Shoot. I needed to try again. I searched around for another daisy on the grassy spot where I was perched. I was sitting underneath the bleachers Hank had set up for the picnic. It was cool in the shade and the best part was that no one could see me eat.

I was on my second hotdog and I planned to have a third. Beyond the bleachers they were all playing tag football. Naturally Garrett was the quarterback. Of course he was the quarterback, because he was the best ever.

In everything.

Which was why I needed to find another flower that I could pluck that would end with him loving me instead of not loving me.

I took a bite of my hotdog and mustard squirted out onto my shirt. Shoot. Mom would be mad about that. She would be mad I was eating hotdogs at all. She called things like burgers and dogs common food.

What she didn't know was that they were delicious. And eating common food was pretty much the only thing that made me happy. So I ate a lot of it. Especially today.

Hank had said Dylan might show up today for the barbecue. Hank had invited him and he thought his mother would let Dylan come this time.

But at the last minute Dylan called to say he couldn't make it, which is what usually happened. I don't know why I ever expected him to come when he had only visited the ranch that one summer.

Bea had been right. I shouldn't have let myself get too close. Dylan wasn't like Garrett. Who came to every party he was invited to and who was always nice to me.

I heard the ruckus on the field and saw Ronnie waving and calling for the ball. Garrett threw directly to her, but it sailed right through her hands and into the bleacher seats. The people sitting on top, mostly Hank and his buddies, scrambled out of the way and the ball actually fell through and practically dropped into my lap.

Knowing it was my chance to talk to Garrett, I leaped at it. I got up with the ball in one hand and my hotdog in the other. I came out from under the bleachers and started running. We were using the flat land beyond the open pen and large stable building as the football field, but at that moment it felt as if I had a mile to run. Halfway to Garrett, I tripped.

I could hear Hank and his friends laughing.

"I think she needs to run more and eat less hotdogs, there, Hank," one of them said with a huge roaring laugh at his own joke.

I ignored them all and got up. Garrett had already reached me and was giving me a hand. He was scowling at the men still laughing on the bleachers.

The hotdog was ruined so I dropped it on the field.

"Here you go, Garrett," I said, a little out of breath, as I handed him my prize.

He smiled at me and I got lost in his green eyes like I always did whenever I saw him. He was fifteen, and too old, and technically I wasn't even allowed to like boys yet, but I liked him. I had always liked him. I was so lucky it was his family's ranch that bordered Hank's property to the north.

"You're the best, Brin."

Brin. I liked that, too. That's what Dylan had called me that summer. I shrugged and giggled a little in response.

"Sure you don't want to play?"

I shook my head. I couldn't throw or catch. I wasn't good at any of that kind of stuff and I didn't want him to see how much slower I was than Bea at running. Bea always won any race between us.

"I like watching," I said.

"Yeah, you're a watcher, all right. You're rooting for me, though, right?"

I nodded.

"Okay, go be my best cheerleader."

I sighed and ran off the field. I was Garrett Pine's best cheerleader. It made me so happy I didn't even want another hotdog.

There were, however, cupcakes. Couldn't miss out on those.

SABRINA

High School—Start of Freshman Year

"I don't understand. I thought her family was so rich. Why wouldn't they send her to fat camp or something?"

I pretended not to hear the girls whispering about me as I passed their lunch table with my tray of food.

It was fried chicken fingers and french fries. More common food, as my mother would tell me. Certainly nothing healthy at all. But it's not like anyone at home cared enough to make lunch for me and, well, I guess I didn't care, either.

I was headed for an empty table in the back of the lunchroom. Hopefully where I could just sit and eat and read without anyone saying anything nasty.

That hope was quickly dashed when the three boys, sophomores I was pretty sure, stepped in front of me.

"You might consider a salad the next time," one of the boys said.

"Or at least a fucking piece of fruit," another snorted.

"Hey, you three dipshits got a problem with me?"

I turned around when I heard the familiar voice, but I couldn't believe it was actually him. Garrett Pine. My lifelong crush. Well, my crush for as long as I had known what a crush was.

"No, Garrett. No problem with you," said the boy who had told me to eat fruit.

"Well, it sounds like you've got a problem with Brin. People who have a problem with Brin have a problem with me. Get it?"

Uh, yeah, they got it. Garrett was a senior. The quarterback of the football team. The most popular guy in school. And right now he was here, sticking up for me. But that's what he always did.

The three sophomores looked like they were going to poop themselves.

I thought I might faint.

"Yeah, sure, Garrett. Sorry," one of them mumbled to me. Then they were gone.

I sat down at the empty table and Garrett sat next to me. So... fainting was still an option.

I picked at my fries and he opened up a lunch bag and pulled out a sandwich. That's right. Technically, I was having lunch with Garrett Pine. Me, fat Sabrina King, and Garrett. I could barely contain myself I was so nervous.

"You didn't have to do that," I said, feeling like I should have done a better job sticking up for myself.

"Yes, I did. I'm so sick of it. People being assholes to each other. What do they get out of that?"

I shrugged my shoulders.

"Don't let it get inside your head. Be confident in who you are."

Was he joking? I was a fat freshman. That was nothing to be confident about.

"Okay," I said. Because it wasn't like I was going to defy him.

After a few man-sized bites, he finished his sandwich and packed up his stuff. I wish I had said more. Been funny. Anything. I was too busy having a near heart attack to manage actual words.

"I mean it, Brin. Shake off the haters. Own your shit. No matter what it is."

"Right. Thanks, Garrett."

"See you around."

Well, I would be seeing him, I thought. Because the one advantage of being a freshman was that for the whole year I got to go to school with my lifelong crush.

SABRINA

Freshman Year—Winter

It was between classes and I was coming back from the bathroom. I was walking down the school hall, minding my own business, which is how I had decided to navigate high school. Head down, keep my nose in my books (my romance novels, not my textbooks), and just avoid the people around me. It wasn't exactly *owning my own shit*, as Garrett had once told me to do, but I found if I didn't bother them, they mostly didn't bother me. Mostly.

I was still a King and that meant people thought they knew things about me. So the idea that I didn't fit in the King family still made me a target for some. But I was dealing.

What I was dealing with less well was the fact that Dylan was officially gone. Hank told us he'd enlisted in the army as soon as he turned eighteen. It wasn't like we had seen him much. Still, it felt like there was this person who had been in my life who was now suddenly gone from it.

The army might has well have been Mars.

Bea pretended like she didn't care, and Ronnie just said he had to do what he had to, but still it felt a little like...he was leaving us for good. I wondered what might bring him back. I stopped when I heard voices.

The hallway should have been clear, but there was clearly something going on around the corner.

"Let me go!"

"Make us, fag."

"I'm not even!"

There were two of them against one. I knew who they all were —Dusty Creek's one high school wasn't that big. Kevin, who was being pinned to his locker, was in my class. The other two were juniors. Buddy and Fitz. They lived to terrorize anyone who they thought strayed from the straight and narrow path of a true Texan.

Kevin didn't like guns and he wore skinny jeans. Enough said.

I thought about Garrett and that day he'd stood up for me back in September. He'd been so angry that people felt the need to treat each other like this. Suddenly I felt that anger, too. I could turn around and walk away from it all. Stepping in would only invite trouble. Trouble I most likely couldn't handle.

But Kevin looked more than annoyed. He looked scared.

"Hey," I said, rounding the corner. "Leave him alone!"

"Oh, if it isn't Princess Fat Ass," Buddy said. "Take a hike. This doesn't concern you."

"Yes, it does. Kevin is a friend and you guys are being jerks. Just let him go." He wasn't really a friend. I didn't really have friends. Hard to make them when all you wanted to do was avoid people.

Then Fitz, who was pretty big for a junior and really shouldn't be calling anyone else fat, started to walk toward me. I could have run, but I didn't.

"You know you're considered the ugly King sister," he sneered.

I did.

I shrugged my shoulders. "Yes, but I'm also the funniest, so there is that. You're not going to do anything with me watching. So just let Kevin go."

Fitz looked like he was going to retaliate when suddenly he stopped. Buddy took his hands off Kevin and stepped back. Kevin stumbled but thankfully he didn't fall on his butt.

The two juniors turned their backs and walked past me, and Kevin just gave a chin nod in my direction and took off down the hallway. Not for nothing, but he did rock his skinny jeans.

I thought that had gone remarkably well. I mean, I did it. I stood up to two bullies and they backed down!

I gave myself a little fist pump and made my way back to class.

SABRINA

Freshman Year—Spring

I knew they would be here. Caroline was so predictable. Quietly I made my way to the top level of the bleachers. School was out for the day. The football field was empty now that it was winter and the season was over. No one around except Caroline and...her boyfriend.

My someday-in-the-future boyfriend, Garrett.

I knew I had as much chance of getting Garrett to go out with me as I did of becoming a world-famous model. But a girl could dream.

Fantasize.

Stalk.

They were making out now, and it hurt a little. Because, as silly as it was, I considered Garrett to be mine.

Which was ridiculous. I knew that. It was just that from the moment I met him he'd been my hero. Because he didn't see the fat girl or the ugly sister. He just saw me. He was best person I knew. And I had to believe that it all meant something.

That we were meant to be something.

He'd started dating Caroline a few weeks ago, and it broke my heart because she had a reputation in school for being totally slutty. And not just she'd-slept-with-a-few-guys slutty, because that was slut shaming and not cool. No, the rumor with Caroline was that she didn't necessarily stop sleeping with one guy before she started sleeping with another one. She also liked older guys. Like, super old. There was one rumor that she was seeing a ranch hand who was TWENTY-EIGHT! That was practically thirty, which was totally ancient.

Except now all the rumors were about her and Garrett, and how they liked to spend time under the home team bleachers when school was out.

So here I was. And they were below me and I could hear them kissing.

God, what a high that would be. Kissing Garrett. Feeling his lips on me, his hands on me. I didn't know much about actual sex. Just everything I knew from my romance novels— which seemed like a lot, but it wasn't real.

It's not like I could talk to my mother about it. I couldn't talk to her about anything. Not when she was always so disgusted with me.

Hank certainly wasn't any better. There were times I wasn't even sure if he knew who I was.

It was very obvious to me my father had wanted sons.

Hank had gotten three daughters. And Dylan.

But Dylan was in the army now and no one had heard from him all year. After Christmas came and went without a word, I stopped thinking that maybe he still cared about us. That I truly did have a big brother in my life.

Besides, who needed him when I had Garrett? Garrett, who at least knew me.

I suppose I could talk to Ronnie about stuff. My oldest half sister was at least somewhat cool with me when she was around, but it was obvious she cared more about Bea than me. Maybe because Bea was always getting into trouble.

So even though I was supposed to have a brother…he was gone.

Even though I had a mother. I didn't have a…mother.

And even though I had two sisters…I never really felt like I had sisters.

Sisters I could talk to about my feelings for Garrett. Sisters who would understand this complete and total longing I felt anytime I saw him. And the pain of watching him wrap his arms around another girl.

He was playing with her hair now as I lay flat on the bleacher, keeping my limbs from dangling so I could just peek over the edge.

Not that I was hidden from view. Too much of my body spilled over on either side. All they had to do was look up and they would know I was there. But why would they do that when they were too busy making out?

He was cupping her jaw in his hand and brushing her bangs out of her eyes and looking at her…looking at her as if he saw everything about her. It wasn't fair. That was my look.

"Hey, Garrett, you know my parents are out of town. We could go back to my place," Caroline said to him.

Her place! No, not that. It was bad enough that they were making out. If they went back to her place, they would have sex.

That would be one more person who was going to have sex with Garrett before I could. Because, while I knew I couldn't have Garrett now, I had a long-term plan. A plan that involved growing up and becoming someone he would be interested in dating. Like, when I was eighteen.

Realistically I knew that between now and then there were would be other girls in his life. Other women. But I wanted that number to be as small as it could be and I certainly didn't want skanky Caroline to be one of them.

I didn't care that she was beautiful. I only cared that she wasn't good enough for him.

Because Garrett was perfect. Tall, built like the football quarterback he was, dark hair, crazy green eyes that made every girl in school swoon when they saw him. But he was more than hot. He was the best thing a person could be.

He was kind.

Kind and understanding and he didn't deserve Caroline who would sleep with him and then might go back and sleep with the TWENTY-EIGHT-year-old guy.

"Yeah," he said. "That sounds like a plan."

I don't know what came over me. It was like I blanked out and forgot who I was. Forgot everything that made sense.

"*No*! You can't!" I shouted it down to them and then I quickly ran down the bleachers to stop them.

I was out of breath by the time I got to the bottom and the two of them were standing there, holding hands, looking at me like I was crazy.

I might have been a little crazy.

"Were you spying on us?" Caroline demanded.

"Garrett," I panted. "You don't want to do this."

"Brin, what's up?"

Brin. My nickname. The one that made me feel special.

"You can't have sex with her," I told him. Pleaded with him, really.

"Brin..." he started to say, and I could see his face turn red. He didn't feel comfortable with my talking like that. It was too personal. Too in his business. I got that, but it didn't matter.

"She's not good enough for you."

"You fat little piece of shit. What did you just say?"

I let the fat comment roll off me. I had been doing that ever since Garrett had encouraged me. *Own your shit.*

That's what he'd told me to do. It was in that moment I'd decided my weight was my issue and nobody else got to tell me how to feel about it. Not Hank, not my mother. Not the other kids in school. Certainly not Caroline.

"She's cheating on you. Everybody knows it." It was a lie. I didn't know if she was cheating on Garrett. I only knew she had cheated on other guys.

"You bitch!" she screeched. "That's a fucking lie. Garrett. She's lying."

"Brin, what's this about?" He walked up to me then and put his hand on my shoulder, and suddenly I wanted to cry. Because I was too young and too fat and not nearly good enough for him, either.

Because I was lying to him.

"She's not good enough for you," I muttered, my bottom lip trembling.

"Oh, jeez, does the little fatty have a crush on Garrett? Is that what this is all about?"

"Hey, cool it, Caroline. All right?" Garrett barked at her. "Brin, look at me."

I shook my head. I couldn't look at him. I knew that if I did I would seriously lose it.

"It's not cool to spy on people. Or to lie, for that matter."

I nodded. I knew that.

"Garrett, let's just leave."

I stood there while he made his way back to Caroline. Took her hand. She smirked at me as if to show that she'd won the battle.

I suppose she had. They were going to go back to her parents' place. They were probably going to have sex. She was going to get to have him. For a time.

While I was going to have nothing.

"You should run a few laps around the track while you're out here...might do you some actual good," Caroline said over her shoulder as they walked away.

I saw Garrett tug her hand and heard him mutter. "Not cool."

She was a bitch. She wasn't nice or kind, which meant she wasn't good enough for him.

Suddenly I felt this deep well of rage in my stomach. None of this was fair. Not the fact that my dad wanted me to be a boy, or that my mother thought I wasn't good-looking enough to be her child, or that my one half sister hated me and my other half sister had too much going on in her life to really care about me.

That Dylan had just left me.

That Caroline got to have Garrett just because she was older and pretty.

I looked at the track and suddenly the idea of running felt great. Felt freeing. Yes, that was exactly what I wanted to do. I wanted to run. I wanted to run until all this anger and all this hurt went away.

So I did. And I didn't stop until I collapsed.

2

SABRINA

High School—Senior Year—Prom

“And the winner is...of course, Sabrina King! Our new Prom Queen!”

I tried to act like I was surprised. I gasped. I put my hands on my cheeks. I shook my head as if in disbelief. The reality was that I’d known I was going to win. I was the richest, prettiest, and most popular girl in school these days. Something that had taken years, but I’d finally done it.

In my designer gown and seven-hundred-dollar shoes, I went up on the stage that had been set up in the gym for this purpose. I stood in front of the senior class while Mrs. Rugger, the vice principal who had called my name, put a ridiculously cheesy crown on top of my head.

Everyone was clapping and screaming. I was waving back to everyone.

David, my date for the evening was high-fiving his friends. He probably thought he was getting lucky tonight. He was so not getting lucky tonight.

Because I had a plan.

A four-year plan that was going to culminate tonight.

Finally, Garrett Pine was back in Dusty Creek.

He'd gotten a degree in criminology and was now working for the sheriff's department. I had seen him the other day on the street and my heart almost stopped. Then I'd quickly hidden around the corner of a building so he wouldn't see me.

Not that he might recognize me. I was a long way away from the fourteen-year-old fat girl he'd saved from being bullied.

That day when I'd spied on him and Caroline I had been so angry I started running. And I kept running. And any other time I was angry I ran, which was a lot. And it was crazy, because the more I ran, the more weight I lost.

The more weight I lost, the more people wanted to be my friend. Wanted to make out with me. Wanted to have sex with me.

The more weight I lost, the more my mother wanted to hang out with me. Go shopping with me.

Was I the only person who understood how superficial that was?

Being thin didn't make you cool. It didn't make you nice or kind or a good friend. It was like all these people in my life just saw me as a body.

Fat, don't like her. Thin, like her.

They wanted a Barbie doll. So, in a lot of ways, that's what I became. Kind of this character everyone expected me to be, which kept the real me, the awkward fat girl, tucked inside where nobody could see her.

But here was what I didn't do. I didn't judge other girls for the way they looked. I was *nice* to everyone. I made sure no one bullied anyone around me. Ever. If they wanted to be considered one of my posse, they had to be cool to everyone.

So people liked me. The nerds and the jocks. The beautiful and the not so beautiful. The honor students and the special-needs kids. All of them. Because I knew the secret. How a person looked said nothing about who that person was. But how a person looked could mean everything when it came to how they were treated by others.

No, I hadn't wanted Garrett to see me that day on the street. That seemed too insignificant. Our meeting, when it came, had to be an event.

It had to be shocking. It had to be impactful. I had to look my absolute best because I knew there was power in that, especially over guys. Tonight's outfit was perfect. When he saw me he would see the sexy black strapless dress, the killer high-heeled sandals, my thick dark hair that I had paid to have blown out so it was long and shiny down my back. My makeup, also professionally done, to highlight my cheekbones and dark brown eyes. I knew my way around a makeup kit, but tonight it had to be perfect.

It wasn't as if I could invite him to go to the prom with me. He was a college graduate. He would think that was lame. Which meant I had to do something else. Given that he was working as a deputy sheriff, I figured it would get his attention if a crime was committed.

Not a real crime, of course. A fake crime. I was looking for some drama, but nothing too crazy. Just something that might lure Garrett to the school where he would see me again for the first time.

Startle him a little. Shake him loose from his perception of me as a kid. I wanted him to see the woman I was. The person I had grown into, even though part of it was a farce. He didn't need to know that right away.

I walked through the crowd of my fellow juniors and seniors. Smiling, kissing cheeks, laughing at how silly the crown was. Showing off my shoes, which everyone wanted to see. I danced with David, but when he tried to grab my ass I pulled his hand up around my back.

David was okay, but he knew we were just here as friends. I had been totally up front with him about that when he asked me. Because the whole time I knew I had this plan.

I made excuses about heading to the ladies' room and instead found a trash can into which I dropped (sorry, Hank) my very expensive diamond pendant necklace. The plan was to retrieve it, but I didn't want to put it somewhere obvious. As long as I recovered if from the trash before Monday morning it would be fine.

In the meantime...

"Help!" I screamed as I ran back into the gym. "Someone stole my necklace!"

I held my breath as the principal's door opened. I knew it would be him. Not because I had hope, but because I had done my research. This plan hadn't just happened. It was carefully crafted. I knew his shift at the department. Knew that a low-level emergency would warrant the least senior deputy.

When he walked in, I tried not to suck in my breath. He hadn't changed at all. Same dark hair that was never quite tamed. Same build, maybe bigger, only now decked out in a deputy's uniform. He was a cowboy in a cop's attire, and my mouth nearly went dry at the sight of him.

"Thank you for coming, Garrett," Mrs. Rugger greeted him. She was in charge of the matter since she'd been chaperoning the prom.

"No problem, Mrs. Rugger. Good you see you again. So what's the..."

"Hi, Garrett," I said, leaping out of my chair. I pushed my hand at him so he would have to touch me. Have to acknowledge me.

Four years of waiting for this moment. Hundreds of angry miles run. A stylist to make me look my absolute best.

He looked me up and down, which was good, I thought, and then his beautiful eyes scrunched as if he was trying to look at me through some prism.

"Brin?"

I knew he would see me. The me beneath the expensive dress and shoes and makeup. The real me. My heart started to pound against my chest.

"Hi."

He took my hand and shook it. Then he smiled slowly. "You grew up."

"It happens."

He laughed. "Yeah, I guess it does. So, it was your necklace that got stolen?"

"Yes. I don't know what happened. There were so many people, all of us bumping around as we danced. I thought it might have fallen off, but I couldn't find it anywhere. Eventually I realized someone might have slipped it off my neck."

See? Nothing crazy. Just a necklace that I may or may not have lost that someone may or may not have taken. I would need a police report for the insurance, so of course the sheriff's team had to be called.

"Do you have a time frame of when it happened?"

"I can tell you it was after she was crowned Prom Queen," Mrs. Rugger said. "You had it on then."

"Prom Queen, huh?" Garrett said.

"I know. Crazy, right? Fat little Sabrina King..."

"Hey." He stopped me. "You were always too hard on you."

And there it was. His kindness. So warm and comforting you just wanted to curl yourself up in it. One day I would be curling myself into his arms and that would be even better. I knew it.

The door to the principal's office opened and it was one of my classmates. Cindy Bitner. She was screeching that she'd found it and when I saw what was in her hand my heart started to thud, only not the good kind. The oh, my God, I might have a heart attack kind.

No, no, no. This was not part of the plan. He was supposed to offer to drive me home. Explain the lost necklace to my father. We were supposed to have time together to talk. To really get to know each other.

"It was so crazy," Cindy said. "I went to throw out a napkin, but then I lost my clutch in the garbage. So I opened the lid to get it and bam! It was right there! Do you think someone planted it there and was waiting to pick it up later?"

Yes. I think that was exactly the plan.

Garrett took the necklace from Cindy and handed it back to me. "Not usual for a criminal to ditch the goods. Maybe someone panicked and changed their mind."

"Maybe," I said as I took it back.

"It's beautiful," he said. "Almost as pretty as its owner."

I blushed. I had received any number of compliments since I had grown an inch and lost a bunch of weight. Things like my mother saying it was about time. From guys in my class who said things like, *You're hot now, do you want to fuck?* But this was my first from Garrett. Maybe for the first time I believed it.

I put the necklace back on and smiled at him.

"Guess my job here is done. Not really much chance of finding out who did this. Just maybe keep better tabs on your jewelry."

"Thank you, Garrett," Mrs. Rugger said. "Or I suppose I should call you officer."

"You've known me since I was fourteen. I think Garrett is fine. See you around the ranch, I suppose, Brin."

I nodded. It was easier than speaking in that moment. I watched him leave and I thought about my foiled plan. At least he'd seen me looking as nice as I could. Still, there hadn't been nearly enough time to interact.

Maybe next time I would get him out to the ranch. Someone outside the window, maybe? A potential break-in?

I would figure out something. Because Garrett Pine was my destiny. I just knew it.

SABRINA

The King's Land

"I'm sure it was nothing, but I was so afraid. I didn't think it was anything..."

It was early in the evening and I was standing at the door to my home. Garrett was on the patio. I felt a niggle of doubt about this plan, mostly because I felt like was I was establishing a pretty bad pattern of lying to him.

I'm pretty sure lying was not the best way to start off a serious relationship. But in the weeks since graduation I had only seen Garrett a few times in town. My mother was insisting I spend more and more time with her in Dallas.

Now that I was fashionable she wanted to show me off to her friends.

I'd left her with the excuse that I was getting sick, and Jennifer never wanted anything to do with the sick.

Hank was out of town on business. And Ronnie and Bea were off shopping, getting ready for Ronnie's upcoming engagement party.

It was the first time I could ever remember having the house to myself. Well, myself and the servants, but I had conveniently given them the night off.

Trudy had protested until I told her it was my one shot at being the boss in this family so she should take advantage of me.

She'd laughed, and eventually given in and gone to the movies with her husband, Oscar.

Cue mysterious rattling of the back door off the kitchen, which I may or may not have feared was an intruder trying to break in, and a call to the local sheriff's office. Mary, the receptionist had picked up.

Because my one evening alone was a little fortuitous, I'd needed to get somewhat lucky. Which I had. I casually asked if Garrett was on shift and, if he was, if he'd mind stopping by King's Land on his way back to his place because I was afraid I'd heard something.

No big deal. Nobody breaking in. Just maybe someone snooping around the place.

Now he was here, and the truth was, I wasn't sure what to do with him.

"It's not no big deal if you were frightened, Brin. Let me in and I'll take a look around."

"Okay."

Garrett walked inside and I could see him take in the massive, sprawling ranch house. It was funny, but I sometimes forgot how big it was until I saw it through the eyes of someone else.

Hank liked big space and big horns. So the open-plan ranch had as few walls as possible and as many animal heads hung on the walls as possible.

I knew Garrett's family had owned the land north of ours, although I had never been to his ranch.

Hank's place eclipsed any ranch for hundreds of miles, so everything else seemed small in comparison. Even insignificant in some ways, although I could see now it was superficial to think that way. I should have known more about his parents, their operation. I didn't.

All I knew was that the Pines had retired to Arizona last year and Garrett had moved back home and was breeding bulls for the rodeo in addition to his job at the sheriff's office.

"Been a while," Garrett said, walking through the place. "I forgot how...grand it was."

Grand? He meant garish. Jennifer's taste ran toward gilt. I knew that. I'm not sure why, but the slight hurt a little.

"That's how we Kings roll," I said, hiding behind all things King. "Everything is bigger in Texas, including Hank King."

He lifted his chin at that. "So, where did you hear the noise?"

"Oh, this way." I led him through the formal living room with the two massive facing white couches, into the games room, then through the ballroom to the dining room, and from there to the kitchen. There was a sunroom off the kitchen that was meant to be a breakfast room, although no one ever used it. Off the porch was a door.

"It sounded like someone was turning the knob. Trying to get in." I bit my lip and said a silent apology to the god of truth. But this was my destiny, after all. A girl had a right to fight for it.

Garrett opened the door and looked outside. He studied the knob itself. Wiggled it in a way that might have made a sound I might have heard.

"Were you in the kitchen when you heard it?"

Right. Because if I had been in the living room or the games room I wouldn't have heard a thing. However, if I had been in the kitchen, I would have been able to see if anyone was on the other side of the door.

"Just outside. I was coming down for a drink," I said. "Speaking of which, can I offer you something? Hank always has some specialty beers."

I walked over to the smaller drinks fridge and opened it.

"Sorry. On duty."

"Oh, right," I said. "Well, then, something to eat? I made brownies with peanut butter chips in them."

I had spent all day baking until I'd made a perfect batch. They were now perfectly stacked on a piece of china on the kitchen's center island.

"Brownies, huh? Sounds good, but I think I'll have to pass."

"Oh. I have chips and hummus." I walked over to the fridge and started pull stuff out onto the counter. "Salsa and guacamole, too."

"Brin."

I turned at the sound of his voice.

"This is a police call," he said. "You don't have to entertain me."

"I was just trying to be nice."

He opened the back door and walked outside. Looking for footprints, maybe, or some sign that someone had been there. After a few minutes he came back inside.

"I don't see anything. Doesn't look like anything was disturbed."

"Oh," I said. "I guess it could have been the wind or something."

He nodded. "Well, if that's all…"

Shit, shit, shit. The whole point of this drama was to spend time with him. Get to know him. For him to get to know me. How could we be each other's future if we didn't talk more?

"You know my sister is engaged. We're having a big party here. You should come. Everyone's invited. You know Hank, it will be a massive blowout."

Garrett smiled. "Sounds fun."

"I'm just thinking it would be nice to see you. You know, not on an official call or anything. To see you out of your uniform. I mean, not out of it, like completely out of it, just you know…I'm rambling."

Garrett smiled. "Brin," he said softly. "I would like to see you, too, but…"

He wanted to see me. This was my chance. I didn't think, I just pushed my way toward him and grabbed his face. Except when I tried to kiss him, he turned his head and gently pushed me away.

"Brin, no. I'm sorry I should have made it clear. The reason I can't see you is I'm pretty sure my fiancée wouldn't like that very much."

It took a minute for the word to penetrate. Fiancée. What did that mean again? It was a fancy word for...oh, right. Girlfriend you were going to marry.

"I didn't know." Oh, my God. I had just tried to kiss an engaged man! "I'm so sorry."

"Nothing to be sorry about. I met her in college, sophomore year, and that was it for me. I came back home to get things settled at the ranch. She's tying up some loose ends where she's from, but she'll be here in a few days."

But that didn't seem possible. He was *my* destiny. *My* future. How could he belong to someone else?

"Oh." I tried to school my features, but I knew it was pretty useless. He had to see that I was crushed. I couldn't stop my heart from pounding against my chest.

"Brin, you know I think you're a sweetheart. To me you'll always be that girl with the big eyes and my best cheerleader..."

"The fat girl, you mean," I snapped. I needed to get him out of the house before I lost it.

He lowered his eyes. "I'm not good at this. I know that. Listen, if this wasn't...I mean if...I guess if it was your imagination, you don't need me here."

"No. I don't. I'll see you out."

I walked him back through the house until we reached the foyer. Somehow in that time I managed to find an ounce of pride. A smidge of graciousness.

Garrett was engaged to someone.

Garrett was meant for someone else.

My future, the one I had always seen when I thought of him, was suddenly gone. Replaced by this vague fog of uncertainty.

I opened the door and he stepped past me and stopped.

"Brin..."

“I really prefer Sabrina,” I said around a swallow. “You know, eighteen and all. Time to grow up.”

He nodded. “Okay. See you around, Sabrina.”

“I meant what I said, though. You should come to the party. Bring your fiancée?” I left it as a question.

“Betty. Her name is Betty.”

I smiled big and false. “Bring Betty. We can show her how the Kings do it in style.”

3

SABRINA

The King's Land—Engagement Party

The lights were sparkling. The champagne was flowing. I was wearing Vera Wang and Jimmy Choo. A couple of Cartier classics. There was media out in front of the property, as some of Hollywood's elite would be in attendance. Hank liked starlets and starlets liked Hank's money.

It was everything that Hank wanted. I had no idea if it was what Ronnie wanted.

The ballroom was filled with people dancing. Hank had hired a ten-piece band. Every nook in the house seemed to be filled with guests. Two hundred, maybe three hundred people.

But there was only one guest who mattered to me. Garrett looked handsome in a suit. And next to him, Betty looked...cute. A simple black dress, no-name shoes. A shiny, if tiny, diamond on her ring finger. A piece of jewelry I was so jealous of it nearly stole my breath.

She was blonde and petite. Like Caroline, now that I thought about it. Had I ever stood a chance with Garrett? Did he only like short, cute blondes?

"Brin!"

I smiled as he lifted a champagne glass in the air. Slowly I walked over to them, making sure I used every ounce of everything I had been taught about posture and gait. My mother had insisted on lessons when she realized I had the potential to be something other than just a fat kid. For once I was grateful for her interference in my life.

If I couldn't have Garrett, I needed to know that I had least changed his perception of me, from the fat girl to Sabrina King.

Betty was practically coming out of her shoes, she was so excited.

"Garrett," I said, reaching out my hand toward him. "Welcome." He took it and shook it like I had confused him with my formality.

"Please introduce me to your fiancée."

"Brin..."

"Sabrina," I corrected him with a smile.

"Right. Sorry. Sabrina, this is Betty. Betty, this is Sabrina King."

Betty squealed. "Oh, my gosh, I'm so excited to meet you. I've seen you on TMZ, like, so many times. And then your whole family was featured in *People*."

"Yes. We're happy to have you. Feel free to enjoy the night."

"I can't stay too long," Betty said with a shrug. "I have a friend picking me up to take me to work."

"Betty's a nurse," Garrett explained. "She's working a later shift. And I told you I would take you."

"And miss all this? Don't be ridiculous. I insist you stay and party vicariously for me."

I nodded. A nurse. Yes. Of course she would be something virtuous. While I was...nothing.

"But I couldn't miss a chance to see The King's Land and meet you, so I had to come for a little bit. I had no idea you were Garrett's neighbor."

"I didn't have a chance to ask the other night. How are your parents, Garrett?" I asked politely. As any uninvolved but gracious host would do.

"They're good. Settled now in a retirement community in Arizona. Thanks."

"Well, I hope you'll excuse me. I see Jennifer Lawrence and Emma Stone just arrived, and I would like to greet them personally."

"Oh, my gosh! Garrett did you hear that?"

She was screaming in his ear and tugging on his arm. He was smiling down at her. They were both obviously thrilled with each other. A happy couple.

A broken heart.

"I'll leave you to it."

~

GARRETT

I pulled at my tie a little, which felt like it was strangling me. I had one hundred percent not wanted to be here tonight. Forget that I wasn't a massive crowds guy. Forget that I didn't need to rub shoulders with the muckety-mucks. I had no doubt things would still be awkward with the one person I did like at The King's Land. But when I'd mentioned the invite to Betty, she had practically lost her shit.

I suppose for people not from around here, meeting the Kings was a big deal. Having grown up with our place adjacent to theirs, to me they were just the Kings. Rich, sure. Garish. Yep.

But they threw good barbecues, and the people of Dusty Creek were always invited.

"Garrett, can you get me another glass of champagne? Oh, and caviar! Lots of caviar. Like, a whole plate of it."

I laughed. "Betty, do you even like caviar?"

"I have no idea, but it's rich-people food and I want to try it."

"Okay. But should you have another drink if you're going in to work soon?"

"It's okay. It's just champagne. One more."

"You're okay staying here?" I asked. The buffet was in the dining room area and this place was too crowded for both of us to maneuver back there.

"Uh, yes. I'm just going to stand here and goggle at everyone around me."

"They're just people, Betty."

"Sabrina King is *not* just people, Garrett!"

I left to fetch Betty what she wanted. I wasn't about to contradict her, but Brin King was the epitome of "just people." I'd known her as a girl. I knew the heartache this family had doled out to her on a regular basis, just because she'd been a little chubby.

She wasn't that now. I found myself looking around the room and spotting her talking to some old man who was trying to wrap his arm around her waist to pull her closer to his side. She resisted and the man pulled tighter. I was about to charge in, but she carefully extracted herself from the situation with a gracious smile and moved on to the next circle of guests.

Brin King. Wow. When I had seen her that night at the prom I had been so...proud. Not because she'd lost weight or turned out to be this beautiful young woman...but Prom Queen. That meant she also had to be popular. That the other kids at school liked her.

Okay, maybe there had been other thoughts besides pride, but I wasn't going to think about that too closely.

I remembered, clear as day, when I'd come upon her standing up to Buddy and Fitz while they had some kid pinned against the locker. They were thugs, but fortunately they'd also been on the football team. When they saw their captain approach, all it had taken was a look and they'd stopped what they were doing and taken off.

Brin hadn't known. She'd given herself a fist pump and I'd had to bite my lip to keep from laughing.

I was glad I had done that. Glad that I made her feel like she could do things like stand down bullies on her own.

Where was she? Oh, there. Geezus, it was like you couldn't miss her. In this room filled with actresses and people dressed to the nines, she stood out like a shiny star. Poised. Gracious. Beautiful.

I had smashed her a little bit the other day. I always knew she'd had a crush back in high school, but surely, after all this time...

Then it occurred to me. The necklace. Had that been some kind of stunt? Like the noises she'd heard at the ranch?

Like the time she told me Caroline had cheated on me? She had been right about that. I'd found out she was sleeping with some ranch hand and dumped her ass.

Had all of that been to get my attention?

I couldn't say it wasn't flattering...

Where was she... oh. There, she was. She was telling a story, and whatever it was must have been hilarious because everyone around her was laughing.

Wait, what was I supposed to be doing?

Betty. Champagne and caviar.

Shit. I shook my head and focused on my task. Pushing through the people, I brought back a reasonable amount of caviar and a glass of champagne that she practically gulped.

Betty was cute. Betty was real people. Betty was nice and steady. She'd make an excellent ranch wife. I shouldn't have been thinking about how beautiful Brin was. It felt like a betrayal. *I* had always been a one-woman man. I had committed to Betty and she was going to be my wife. My future.

Which, in some ways, made me a little irritated with Brin. If she hadn't tried to kiss me the other night I might have never considered her in that way. But there had been a second, a brief second, when I couldn't help but wonder what it might be like to kiss her back.

That was wrong. So wrong. Betty didn't deserve that and I was going to scrub it from my memory.

If Brin remained on The King's Land, she would just be a neighbor. An old friend, hopefully. Nothing more.

I watched Betty bite into a cracker with black fish eggs piled on top. Her whole face crinkled into a look of horror.

"Told you." I laughed. "Just because it's rich doesn't mean it's good. I, for one, know Brin King's favorite food is hotdogs."

Betty took another swallow of champagne and actually swished it around in her mouth before she swallowed. "Don't be ridiculous, Garrett. Sabrina King hasn't eaten anything outside of a vegetable or piece of fruit in years. Look at her."

Where was she? I craned my neck. She turned and caught me looking. I smiled, but she ducked her head and walked away.

SABRINA

I did my hostess duties for the rest of the night with a heavy heart and feeling so stupid. Garrett really was nothing more than a childhood crush, then a high school crush. But now it felt...different.

There had been this certainty inside me about him, always. When I was a teenager and thought he was the best person I could know. The person who would always have my back.

But now, when I was finally old enough and attractive enough to gain his attention…

It was too late.

Betty had beaten me to him.

Suddenly the house was too warm. The people were suffocating me. It was like I couldn't breathe the air anymore. I made my way through the throng of guests out to the front patio and down the driveway a bit. Not too close to the gate, where the paparazzi lay in wait for a hint of drama.

I watched a car pull in and stop. This was odd for several reasons. The car in question was a mid-size sedan. Not anything special. Nothing like the Mercedes, Maseratis and Hummers that littered the front lawn.

In fact, it was so unspectacular it made me wary that it was a journalist trying to sneak into the party.

Then I saw a figure running down the driveway toward the car, one hand waving. I was far enough into the dark on the edge of the front lawn that it was doubtful I could be seen, but the moonlight showed off the blonde in the black dress.

Betty.

Of course. It was the friend she worked with who was picking her up. Except when the large man got out of the driver's seat, it took me a second to picture this guy as a nurse. Which was probably sexist of me. I mean, really what year was it… OH MY GOD!

Betty had leaped into the guy's arms and was kissing him. Like, *kissing him*, kissing him.

Without thinking, I ducked down and started to move closer to them. At least within hearing range.

"Luke, stop," she said panting and pushing him off a bit. "He might see."

"I don't give a fuck." The ominous Luke made his point by spitting on the ground at her feet.

"I'm just looking for the right time," Betty insisted. "Now that I'm here…I'll figure it out."

"You've been figuring it out for months. I'm tired of this shit. Tell him it's over and let's get on with it already."

"I will. I will. Soon. I promise. Can we just go? We've got the whole night. He thinks I'm working the night shift at the hospital."

"I got us a room."

"You're the best, babe."

I watched as she climbed into the passenger seat of the car. Watched as Luke made a three-point turn in the driveway and drove back through the gates with Betty.

Garrett's fiancée.

I looked around, hoping to see that someone else had seen that and known what it meant. Sadly, I was alone. I thought about charging back up the house to tell him, but that wasn't exactly news I imagined he wanted to hear.

That his fiancée had been cheating on him. For months!

And did I have to do it, anyway? It sounded like Betty was about to break up with him any day.

Instantly I smiled. All hope was not lost. Garrett was going to need someone to console him after the breakup, and I planned to be just that person.

I would be so loyal to him he would forget Betty ever existed!

I was back, and when I stepped back into the house I felt like a prisoner who had just been granted a reprieve.

SABRINA

Two weeks later

I stopped in front of the window of the diner downtown. I could see it was filled, but that wasn't what caught my attention. I watched as Garrett slid out of the booth and then bent over to kiss Betty before heading to the counter to pay the bill.

It had been two weeks since I saw her with the man she called Luke. The man she'd made out with. The man she'd gone to a hotel with. Two weeks and she hadn't broken up with Garrett yet.

Two weeks where he was still obviously being duped by his seeming sweetheart who, in fact, was a horrible, lying bitch.

Who could possibly cheat on Garrett? Why would anyone *want* to cheat on Garrett?

It made no sense. Not that I wasn't grateful. The fact that Betty was cheating on him and intended to end things meant I was going to get another shot at Garrett. But when? How long did this go on? More importantly, how long did I *let* this go on?

After all the drama with Ronnie taking off and canceling the wedding, I'd had to focus on my family. Ronnie was gone. Bea was distraught. Hank was pissed. My mother had left to go shopping, there was a big surprise. I was trying to hold everyone together and failing miserably at it. Ronnie was the center of this family, not me!

I had thought that by now Betty would have done it and broken the engagement. But she hadn't.

What if she didn't? What if she was just stringing Luke along for the ride?

Garrett had to know.

He walked out of the diner and stopped when he saw me.

"Hey, Brin. Sorry, Sabrina. Any word from Ronnie?"

I shook my head.

"Do you know why she freaked out and called off the wedding?"

Again, I shook my head. I knew the town was talking about it. It was supposed to have been the wedding of the century. Now it was gone. Just like that.

"Garrett, do you have a second?"

"Sure. I'm heading back to the station. Can you walk with me? Or should I say, can you walk in those shoes?"

I looked down at my classic Jimmy Choo beige bumps. The way these shoes were designed I could run a marathon in them, but I get why men who worked for the sheriff and raised bulls didn't get that.

I walked beside him, my stomach churning. This was going to be horrible. Awful. What if he lost it? What if he cried?

I would be there for him. No matter what.

"I have to tell you something and it's awful. But I can't not tell you. Not anymore."

"Okay. This sounds ominous."

We reached the station, which was just a block down from the diner. We stopped in front of the steps that would lead us inside, but I didn't think Garrett would want to hear this news in front of his colleagues. It was going to be upsetting enough. I don't know that I would want someone to see me in this situation.

"Hey there, Garrett." A deputy walked out of the station and took the steps at a jog. He smiled at me. "Why look, it's little Sabrina King. What happened this time Sabrina? Another lost necklace? Break-in? Maybe you've got someone following you."

He laughed and I blushed.

"Cool it, Dave," Garrett said.

"Whatever you say, Garrett." Dave chuckled a little more then got into the squad car that was parked in front.

"Sorry about him. He's an ass."

"It's okay. This is...this is important. That night at the party, Betty said a friend was coming to pick her up at the house."

"Another nurse, yeah."

"Well I was outside on the front lawn getting some air and I saw someone drive up. It was a man. A large man and they...well they...they kissed. Like, seriously made out. And then Betty said..."

"Brin," Garrett interjected. "Stop. Stop right now."

"No, but I have to tell you. He told her to break up with you and..."

"Brin." This time it was more of a bark. His face was tight and he looked genuinely pissed. Not at the situation, but at me. "Enough. You've been pulling this shit for years and it's got to stop. I get it. You have a crush on me. Get over it. No more stunts. No more lies. Geez, this is Caroline all over again."

I shook my head "I'm not lying. He was there. His name was..."

"I'm done, Brin," he said, cutting me off. "Done listening. You're embarrassing yourself and it has to stop."

The breath whooshed out of me. "You don't believe me."

"No. I don't. I don't buy that someone took your fancy necklace and dropped it in the trash. I don't believe that someone was breaking into your house the other night. No one around here would be stupid enough to take on The King's Land security. Now, are we done here? I've got a job to do."

"She's not good enough for you," I muttered.

"Well, she's not a liar, Brin. Sorry, Sabrina. You Kings, you're all so fucking sure of yourselves and your money. You just assume you can have whatever you want. I thought you were different. I thought you were sweet. But now I can see you're just as manipulative as your mother. Nothing better than a cowboy princess in her fancy shoes. Grow up, Sabrina. Get a fucking real life."

I watched him take the stairs and slam the station door behind him.

Pissed. Angry. All of it directed at me.

The worst part wasn't the pain of knowing I was never going to be with Garrett. The worst part was knowing the pain he was eventually going to face. Because it would kill him to know that he was being cheated on, and it would kill him again once he learned I was right about it.

I looked around main drag of this small Texas town and thought there was nothing here for me.

Ronnie, my only ally in the house, was gone. Mother hadn't stuck around. It was doubtful Hank would care if I left.

I thought about getting out of there. I thought about getting out of Texas altogether.

So that was my plan. Leave and continue to be the thing everyone thought I was.

Nothing more than a cowboy princess.

4

SABRINA

Five Years Later—LA Studio

"You can't be serious," my agent, Darleen, said.

"Deadly," I said with only a hint of irony.

"Sabrina." Sam, the executive producer of the show, tried to cajole me. "The emails are scary. No one is suggesting otherwise. But you're in the third year of a hit reality TV show. You can't just walk away from *Cowboy Princess*."

"I'm the star, right?"

"Yes! You are the star. You are the reason the show has so many fans. It's a goldmine. You've built a brand. You have a presence on every social media out there."

Not anymore, I didn't. I was shutting all my accounts down.

"If it's my show, and we're here today negotiating a new contract, then I get what I want. What I want is out. I've already run this by my family attorney, and Madison agrees that I have no legal obligation to renew."

Darleen leaned into me so that only I could hear her. "Excellent move. They have to up your salary per episode now."

I turned to her, furious. I was so tired of this. So tired of no one listening to me. What sucked about that was that I had done this to myself. I had become this *thing*. This character. This Cowboy Princess. And no one thought I had a brain anymore.

"This isn't a trick, or a move, or a strategy. I'm tired of having cameras in my life twenty-four seven while I go about doing absolutely nothing. The stalker, whoever he is, just solidified my position. I'm tired of LA. I'm tired of this life. I don't want to be a target anymore."

"So, what?" Sam asked. "You go back to shopping and partying in Dallas full time instead of part time? Is that really any different?"

I knew I wanted to go home. Even though I wasn't sure why.

Hank was dead. Ronnie and Clayton I guess were getting back together. Which meant she was spending more time at Clayton's place back in Dallas. Bea was doing whatever Bea did, but she hadn't stayed long at The King's Land.

But something about the idea of home right now just felt right. Like I needed to touch base before I could figure out what came next.

I suppose the worst had already happened. Hank was dead, his daughters disinherited. Although I assumed with Ronnie agreeing to marry Clayton that meant he would at least help out Bea. That was, of course, assuming Dylan didn't come home to claim the estate.

He hadn't shown up yet and it had been weeks since Hank died. Ronnie was the only one who had his email address and she was saying he hadn't even responded. No one thought he wanted the inheritance, but that kind of money wasn't something you could just walk away from.

And if he didn't come back? If he did turn his back on all of his sisters? Well, then, I supposed it wouldn't be much different than what he'd done for the last ten years.

It was like everything was suddenly shaken loose in my life, and it made me think, maybe for the first time since I left Dusty Creek.

Was this it? Was this my life?

Because it seemed so empty.

"I don't know what I'm going to do when I get home," I said. I had some savings that would see me through for a while. Maybe now was the worst time to be walking away from the show, with everything so up in the air regarding the inheritance. But these last weeks had been nothing short of horrifying...

And then there was Felix.

"I know I'll feel safe for the first time in weeks and that's worth a lot to me," I finished.

"How many times have I told you?" Sam railed. "These cyber stalkers never do anything serious. Emails, tweets, Facebook messages. It's all behind a computer where they are safe."

"And the dead cat left outside my home?"

That had been the last straw. Felix wasn't mine. He'd been a feral cat that hung out in the woods behind my house in the Hollywood Hills. I kept a food dish in the backyard for him, for when he'd failed in his hunt. That was all. Not really a pet, not mine.

His neck had been broken, his body laid on my doorstep.

Because of my fame, he had suffered.

In that moment I knew I was over it.

"Another stunt. Something to rattle you. You don't even know if it was the same guy. Could be some fan who thought it would make it on to the show."

I hadn't allowed it. I didn't want to give any more attention than this person was already getting with the various Hollywood "news" shows reporting that I was the apparent victim of a stalker. Thank God Ronnie and Bea both hated those types of shows.

No, just like Hank's death and funeral, and returning to The King's Land, there were some parts of my life I wasn't willing to share.

"I'm sorry, Sam. Sorry Darleen. I get why this is important to you both, it's just not important to me anymore, and I have to believe people would start to notice that and stop watching."

I got up even as they continued to protest, but I was done listening.

I felt good. I felt strong. Confident in my decision.

I also felt like I needed pedicure... but that was typical for me.

~

SABRINA

Dallas—Katy Trail

As the song ended I started to slow my pace until finally I was walking. I took the buds out of my ears and let my breath return to normal.

The hiking trail that ran through the middle of Dallas next to an old rail line was pretty empty at this time of morning on a workday. Still, there were a handful of tourists who had maps of the trail in their hands. Some mothers taking their kids out in strollers. An older gentleman walking his mutt.

It had been the perfect place to escape to after brunch with the girls.

Ronnie and Bea were worried about me, I knew. So much that Bea had driven all the way from Austin just to meet up with us. But I wasn't about to tell them the things the stalker had done so far. Bea would most likely think I was making it up or exaggerating. Ronnie would only double down on the worry, and she had enough on her plate with Clayton.

Instead, I'd asked about the wedding plans she'd made so far and she'd looked at me like I had two heads. I had given her a brief outline of what she needed to be doing now to hit a June wedding, and I swear, all the color had run out of her face.

All in all I continued to play my part as the Twinkie sister. Someone who didn't take anything too seriously.

Although Bea had been shocked I was leaving the TV show. I thought about how she'd reacted.

"But you loved being the Cowboy Princess," Bea said.

"Of course I did," I lied. *"But now Ronnie is going to marry Clayton, which means we're not about to lose everything, so I don't really* need *it anymore. The show was getting too stifling. I think I want to travel."*

"You hope *you don't need it anymore,"* Bea said ominously. *"Nothing is official yet."*

"Dylan's not coming back," Ronnie insisted. *"And Clayton promised me he would take care of us. All of us."*

"You don't know that he's not coming back," Bea said. *"Worse, you don't know how Dylan would treat us if he* did *come back. What were we to him but one summer?"*

"That makes me sad," I said. *"If that's all we were to him."*

Bea snorted. *"Whatever. So you're going back to Dusty Creek? That's your idea of traveling?"*

I shook off the memory. Bea was one of the few people in my life who'd always understood there was a contradiction between what I said and what I did.

Still, I was glad I had come back to Dallas first to let them know I was going back to The King's Land and that I was officially done with the show. I also had to tell all my "friends" in the area that they would no longer be my B-list backups.

Jackie and Rachel were cool. They had great taste and they looked good with me when we shopped and even better as a distraction for guys who would try to pick me up only to leave with one of them.

We'd had fun, but I didn't think I would miss hanging out with either of them. They were trust fund babies who, like me, were always looking for a distraction.

They would find somebody else to distract them.

Tomorrow, though, I would head back to The King's Land and start to get my shit straight.

I was young. I was maybe or maybe not rich. There wasn't anything I couldn't do.

So, why can't you figure out what you want *to do?*

I shook my head at my inability to answer my own question, and that's when I saw him.

He was thirty, maybe forty feet ahead of me. Not walking. Just stopped at the end of the trail. His face was covered by a black hoodie, but I got the sense that he was young. Lean, but definitely a guy. I don't know what it was—the lack of dog, the lack of a map. No phone, no buds in his ears.

Just a stillness. A sense that he was watching me.

Every hair on the back of my neck went up and without even thinking I turned and started running as fast as I could down the trail. I looked over my shoulder and saw he'd started to run after me. I didn't think then. I put my head down and sprinted as fast as I could.

I saw two women with some preschool kids around their legs walking farther along up the trail and I screamed.

"Help me!"

Immediately they stopped and turned. The one woman picked up her child, the other moved her kid behind her.

"I'm sorry, I'm sorry but he's following me..."

I turned and pointed behind me, but when I did he was gone.

"He was...he was running after me."

The two women seemed stunned but as soon as they realized

there was no immediate threat they patted my arm as if to comfort me.

"Do you want us to call 911?" the woman holding her child asked me.

I took my phone out of the armband where I wore it for jogging. I could do that. I could call 911. But what would be the point? A man in a black hoodie had been on a running trail, running, and then he disappeared.

I was letting the stalker get to me. There was no way he would have followed me to Dallas. I was being jumpy.

I shook my head. "No, I must have...overreacted. Sorry if I scared the kids."

"It's all right, honey. Better to be safe than sorry," said the other woman. "Do I know you? Because you look very familiar to me."

"Oh, wait," the other woman said. She had put down her child now that the coast was clear. "You're the Cowboy Princess! Oh, my gosh! Tammy, it's her. Sabrina King. We watch your show all the time!"

I smiled.

"Can we get a picture?" The woman named Tammy was already taking out her phone.

Sure. Why not? After all, I hadn't really been chased by a threatening man in a dark hoodie. Had I? I gave them my best TV smile and held my pose as they snapped a selfie with me.

I couldn't get back to The King's Land fast enough.

GARRETT

Pine's Ranch

I walked through the door to the clean scent of lemon. It was my cleaning lady's day to visit and I always loved how the place smelled after she'd been here. I took off my utility belt and firearm and laid it down on the table in my foyer.

The plan was to grab a shower, have a cold beer, and heat up whatever Juanita had left me in the fridge.

The other nice perk to my cleaning lady was she loved to cook and she said I was too skinny for a man. She'd made it her mission in life to fatten me up. While I didn't think it was possible, if she wanted to indulge me with some of the finest homemade Mexican food this side of the border, I wasn't going to object.

As I made my way into the living room I turned on the TV, anticipating the basketball game that was going to be on tonight. The sixty-inch wide-screen TV was one of the improvements I had made to the place when my parents gave me the ranch.

Surround sound, big picture. It was a TV system for a man.

I blinked when, instead of sporting news, I was watching a beautiful woman fill up the television.

A beautiful woman I knew.

"Sabrina. What I have in this box is going to scare you so much you're going to scream."

It was Brin in her LA house with some friends who had come over. It wasn't like I actively watched *Cowboy Princess*, but I wasn't necessarily oblivious to it, either. Juanita liked her reality shows on the tube when she came over to clean.

I watched as Brin poured the two women champagne. That seemed like a constant theme on the program. They were always, all the time, drinking champagne. One woman put a box on the granite kitchen counter of Sabrina's swanky LA digs.

"Open it! You have to."

Clearly buying into the gag, Brin scrunched up her nose. Something she'd done even as a kid. She popped the lid off the box and pulled out a shoe.

Seemed like a normal shoe to me, but the look on her face was pure horror.

"What is this?"

"They're from the discount rack!"

At which point, she dropped the shoe like it was suddenly burning her hands and ran from the room while her friends laughed hysterically at their own joke.

I got plenty of my shoes off the discount rack.

I was about to change the channel when something scrolling along the bottom of the screen caught my attention. A breaking news tag announced that Sabrina King was leaving LA to escape the threat of a Hollywood stalker.

I snorted. "Yeah. Right." I knew how Sabrina loved her stunts. No doubt this one was an attempt to get the ratings up on her show. Although, if you asked Juanita (I may have asked her once), *Cowboy Princess* was already pretty popular.

On-screen, Brin poked her head around a wall into the kitchen, her face the picture of fear.

"Are they gone? Did you put them away? Is it safe to come back? Because if it isn't, someone is going to have to bring my champagne to me."

I smiled. She really was a goofball.

I shouldn't have been so harsh with her that one time...

Stop!

I put the mental brakes on those thoughts. Because those thoughts led back to Betty, and that place only made me an angry asshole.

I had been an angry asshole for too long.

Unable to look away, I stood there and continued to watch her for a bit. She was still beautiful, but thinner than I remembered from five years ago. Almost frail. Like a stiff breeze could carry her away. I thought someone around her should tell her to eat a damn cheeseburger instead of drinking all that champagne.

I didn't know why I was thinking about her at all.

Didn't she fall into the category of women who had lied to me?

And I hated that category. So much so that I hadn't let a woman into my life other than for a quick fuck. Fuck 'em and forget 'em was my official motto.

Which I suppose made me a *cynical* angry asshole, but I had earned the title the hard way.

Suddenly pissed that I was even thinking about Sabrina, or women in general, I changed the channel to sports and felt a sense of relief.

Which brought with it a little bit of sadness, too. Maybe I was never going to recover from what Betty did to me.

5

SABRINA

Dusty Creek

It had only been a few months since Hank's funeral, the reading of the will, and the whole Ronnie-and-Clayton drama. But it was like I was seeing Dusty Creek for the first time. Had it always been this brown, I wondered? And small?

I drove my silver Mercedes through the main drag and parked in front of The Bar. The least original name for a bar that had ever existed. Still, it was the only one in town and it was the fastest way to spread the news of my return.

It was also a good way to let people know that, if any strangers came to town looking for me, I needed to know about it.

I had almost managed to convince myself that the stalker from LA who'd sent me all those threatening emails wasn't the same person I had seen on the jogging trail in Dallas.

Almost.

If this person was planning on following me to Dusty Creek,

there was no way a stranger in this small town would go unnoticed.

I did a quick check in the rearview mirror and refreshed my lip gloss. I got out of the car and made my way inside. Long narrow space, dim lighting, the smell of fried everything, and a long line of people sitting at the bar watching the big-screen TV.

The bartender was someone I didn't recognize. Not that I came here all that often when I was in town. But I could see the place had changed from the time when Hank would bring us here to eat every once in a while, once he'd deemed we were old enough.

He'd called it bonding time with his girls. We called it sitting at a table with Hank watching him eat fried shit and drink whiskey until eventually he was too drunk to drive home. Fortunately, Ronnie had her license by then.

Yeah. Good times.

I made my way through the place, not oblivious to those who were checking me out. It was Dusty Creek, after all. Most of the customers sitting at the long bar were men and not used to someone dressed like I was walking into their space. Especially alone. It would take a few seconds for them to realize who I was.

"Sabrina King. You home?" I saw the older man sitting on a stool. I'd known Walt growing up. He'd been Hank's foreman for years until he retired.

"Hey, Walt. Yes, for now."

"Good. There should be a King at The King's Land."

"Glad you think so, Walt. And thank your son again for all the help with the horses, with Oscar and Trudy being out of town."

"Making good money," Walt said. "He don't mind it."

I continued until I found an open stool at the end of the bar. Once seated I looked over my shoulder to stare back at the men who were openly watching me. It was best to get this part out of the way.

"Gentlemen."

I got a few mumbles. A few hellos. Everyone in this town knew the King family. Didn't mean they all liked us. What with us owning all the land and having all the money, I suppose.

"What can I get you?" the bartender asked. Then he held up his hand. "I can tell you right now I don't have any goddamn champagne."

"A fan of the show, I see." I was guessing that's why he suspected I might order champagne.

"No."

Clearly not someone who enjoyed idle chitchat. "Okay. White wine? Any kind you have will be fine."

He nodded and went to grab a wineglass. I fiddled with my ponytail and hooked the heels of my expensive shoes on a rung of the stool.

"Hey there, li'l girl," the first man up said. "Aren't you that reality TV something-or-other princess?"

I turned on my stool to face him. I didn't know him by name but he looked familiar. Everyone in Dusty Creek looked familiar. Maybe he worked on one of the cattle ranches in the area.

"I am." I smiled. "Would you like a picture?"

He chuckled and pulled on his oversized belt buckle. "I'll start with a picture and then we'll see where it goes from there, sweetie pie."

I took a deep breath. "First, we have to establish a few things. I'm not a girl, I'm a woman. I'm not a sweetie pie, my name is Sabrina. Unfortunately, I'm not interested in having a conversation with you, but if you would like to take a selfie I'll allow the five seconds to do that before the bartender serves me my wine."

His face changed immediately. "Sounds like you're a snooty bitch. Figures, with Hank King as your father."

"Yes, I suppose it does. So I guess you're not going to want that picture. Byeee." I gave him my famous blow-off wave and smile.

I turned back to face the bar and the bartender was there with my drink.

"Chuck giving you trouble?" he asked.

Chuck, of the large belt buckle, had made his way back to his table where he was telling all his friends right now what bitch I was. It would keep the rest of them at bay. At least for a while.

"Nothing I can't handle. I survived LA and Dallas. I can handle the men from Dusty Creek."

"I'm Jack. Just shout if you need something."

He was about to move on to other customers but I reached out to grab his hand. He stopped, clearly confused by what I was doing.

I let go and took a sip of my wine.

"Just do me a favor will you? Anyone comes into town asking about me or The King's Land, could you give me a heads-up?"

"Expecting trouble?"

No. Because that would be crazy, right? Someone following me all the way here.

"Just taking precautions."

Jack nodded. "The sheriff usually comes in around this time after his shift. I'll let him know."

"Let me know what?"

I stilled at the voice behind me. I couldn't believe I hadn't forgotten it. I couldn't believe it still made my heart race. I couldn't believe...how much I missed it.

I turned and there he was. Still tall and handsome. Still with those amazing green eyes that I had never found in the face of any other man. I knew that, of course. I had seen him at the funeral. I'd known he was there. I had felt him.

Now we were talking. Something we hadn't done since... The memories of our last conversation came crashing down, reminding me I had cried myself to sleep for months after it.

But that had been years ago. I was different from the person I was back then.

At least, I thought I was. More mature, certainly. Stronger, hopefully. Strong enough to face him again.

I cleared my throat and tried to lift my chin without making it look like I was lifting my chin too high in the air. "Hello, Garrett."

"Brin. Sorry...Sabrina. You're back home?"

"For now."

"We didn't talk at Hank's funeral," he said.

Of course we hadn't talked. I had done everything in my power to make sure we didn't talk. I had looked. That's all I had done. Just looked. However, I suppose if I was going to be staying in town for a while, there was no avoiding him. Dusty Creek was too small.

"Things were a little crazy." I offered it as an excuse, although he probably had no idea how true it was.

"It's good to see you."

He smiled as he said it. As if it didn't occur to him that the last time we talked he'd humiliated and crushed me.

"Is it?" I asked.

His face changed then, and the kind smile was suddenly gone. Instead, he was looking at this feet and I thought *Good*. Which felt a little spiteful, but I couldn't help myself.

Of course I knew what had happened. Everyone in Dusty Creek knew it. Garrett Pine had been stood up by his fiancée on his actual wedding day. His family, his friends, the whole damn town except for the Kings had been invited.

And Betty hadn't shown up.

Instead she'd left a letter explaining she was in love with someone else and she was sorry, but she hadn't been able to tell him to his face.

"Look, Brin, I know we left things badly. I imagine you know..."

"I know." I interrupted him. Because, as furious as I was with him, as hurt as I had been by him, he was still Garrett Pine and I didn't want to see him humiliated any more than he'd already been.

She hadn't been good enough for him. Now he knew that, too.

"Anyway," he huffed out. "Obviously, I was wrong about some of those things I said to you."

"Some," I whispered. Because not everything he'd said to me had been wrong. I had to acknowledge that, too.

"Can we put that behind us?"

I nodded. But I was still lying to him. I didn't think I would ever put Garrett Pine behind me. Clearly five years hadn't diminished my attraction to him. Which was really sort of sucky.

I didn't want to be *that woman.* The kind of woman who got stuck on a guy who didn't like her back and couldn't get unstuck. It was freaking pathetic.

I was Sabrina King. I was rich and beautiful, and I had been chased by guys from LA to Dallas for the past five years.

But you didn't let any of them catch you.

"Good. Now, what was Jack going to tell me?"

Oh, crap. I snapped my jaw shut. If I told him what I suspected there was no way in hell he would believe me. Why would he?

"It's nothing," I said. "Just...you know, the whole TV thing attracts some weirdos."

He laughed. "Like your 'stalker.' I saw that on the entertainment news. Who was behind that, anyway? Is that something you have a publicist do? Generate some Hollywood buzz?"

And there it was. He already knew about the stalker situation and he didn't believe it was true.

I was tempted to show him some of the emails. Show him what the man wrote about me. What he wanted to do to me. But, then again, I supposed he would think that was fake too. ,

That my *publicist* killed a cat for buzz.

Suddenly I was sad. Like I hadn't been in a very long time. Which only made me smile harder.

"I have go," I said. I pulled out a twenty from my back jeans pocket and put it on the bar. I waved to Jack so he would notice and then got off the stool. Garrett was forced to move to make room for me or get crushed by the heel of my stiletto. "It was nice to see you again, Garrett."

Not!

"Hey, Brin, wait."

But I didn't want to wait. I didn't want to hear him laugh at the idea that I had a stalker. I didn't want him to call me a liar. Again.

I made my way outside and fumbled getting the key fob out of my jeans pocket. I hit the auto starter so that I could make the quickest possible exit.

But it wasn't quick enough.

"Brin, wait. Hold up." Garrett jogged around to the driver's side were I was getting in. I stopped because I didn't want to make more of a big deal of it than I already had by storming out.

"Look, I didn't mean anything by what I said back there."

On the front seat of my car were sunglasses. I reached down and put them on, taking comfort in the fact that they covered half my face.

"I understand. I really do have to go."

"Okay, but if you need something let me know. Seriously. Anything."

That was a joke. "What I need is for you to believe me. But I think we both know that's never going to happen. See you around, Garrett."

GARRETT

Pine's Ranch

What I need is for you to believe me. But I think we both know that's never going to happen.

I was lying in bed that night and her words kept rolling around in my head. What the fuck had that meant?

Brin damn well knew she had a history of lying to me. A history of phony *events* she had staged to get my attention.

Okay, she hadn't been lying about Betty. Or Caroline. But that was it. The two truths in a sea of lies.

Because she'd had a crush on me.

Which she was obviously over. As if a sheriff from a small town in Texas was any match for the Cowboy fucking Princess.

Besides, it wasn't like I had ever thought about her like that. Sure, yes, I had acknowledged that she'd grown up to be a beautiful woman. And, yes, maybe there had been that moment when I first saw her again in the principal's office, all grown up, and she'd made me catch my breath. But the reality was that the girl I knew was the kid with the big brown eyes always looking up at me longingly.

Certainly not the ridiculously smoking-hot woman in the bar today.

With long dark hair and legs that went on forever. And lips that had been freshly glossed and made for kissing. She was the most intimidating-looking woman I had ever seen in my life.

And when she put those sunglasses on to cover her eyes, it had made me irrationally angry.

Angry that I couldn't look at her anymore. Angry that she was putting up this wall between us.

What I need is for you to believe me...

Why? Why did she need me to believe her? Why had she asked Jack to give her a heads-up if there were any strangers in town looking for her? Of course I had gone back to ask him what they had talked about.

There was absolutely no point in suggesting she had someone stalking her in Dusty Creek. There was no buzz to be had here. Just mud, oil, and cattle, and she knew that.

And I wasn't enough of an egomaniac to think she still had a crush on me and was trying to get my attention again. She hadn't gone to the sheriff with her concerns. She'd gone to the local bartender.

Was it possible her story was legit? If so, that meant I was calling her a liar for the third time when she was telling the truth.

If she was telling the truth.

Shit. She hadn't really said anything. Just TV and weirdos. But the look on her face...

I turned over and looked at the clock on my nightstand. It was after one in the morning and I knew it was doubtful I was going to get any sleep. Instead, I was going to think about Brin and what had made her put on those glasses when she was talking to me.

Because I had almost taken them off her face and broken them.

Which was a bizarre thought to have, but it's not like I could stop it.

I was also going to think about how I was going to approach her again. Because for damn certain I was going to learn what Sabrina King was afraid of.

6

SABRINA

The King's Land—A Few Days Later

There were a lot of things I didn't care for about this place. Mostly the memories of growing up. The one thing I loved, however, was the open space. I was running on Hank's land...or Clayton's land now, I supposed, and it felt like I was alone in the world.

No one to watch me, no one to even think about looking at me. Just me and the open space around me. I ran on the road that was alongside the property just because it was a flat surface, but I might think about mapping out some running trails up in the hills behind the house.

Also there was that access road that led west, toward where Clayton's father lived.

Those two were super confusing, but thankfully Ronnie had come to her senses and put me in charge of the wedding planning. Not only did it give me something to focus on, I could guarantee it would be a fantastic King-like event.

I was heading back now, toward the front of the property, when I saw it. A truck parked outside the gate that led to the driveway. Immediately, I stopped.

I was hot, dripping in sweat, with my unwashed hair in a bad ponytail on top of my head.

In other words, there was no way Garrett could see me like this. And, of course, I knew it would be Garrett. He would have thought about what I said and he probably felt guilty for calling me a liar again. He probably should, but still...

He could NOT see me. Sadly, invisibility was not an option in this moment.

"Hey, Brin," he said, getting out of the cab of his truck. I could see the stenciling along the side that marked it as a County Sheriff's vehicle. I hadn't congratulated him about his promotion from deputy to sheriff. It felt like something the old Sabrina would have done that the new me didn't want to do.

I started walking toward him, my hands on my hips, taking steady breaths as if this was all just part of my normal routine.

When I reached him I stayed far enough away that he couldn't smell me.

"Garrett," I said, not really sure what else to say.

"You run in that?" he asked, pointing at me up and down.

I glanced down. "You mean sneakers, running shorts, and a tank top? Uh, yes."

"Right. Look, I think we got off to bad start the other day. I've been hoping to catch you in town, but I haven't seen you."

"I've been keeping to myself out here," I said, purposefully not saying I had wanted to avoid him.

"Look, if you're expecting trouble..."

"I'm not," I said, cutting him off. "I'm not expecting anything. I'm home to avoid trouble."

"Still, I made it seem like anything going on in your life wasn't real. I didn't mean to do that. I just...I just assumed..."

"I get it, Garrett," I told him. He'd just assumed I was up to my old tricks. I, however, didn't necessarily want to be reminded of what I had done in the past. "You should know, I'm not the same person I was when I left."

At least, I hoped I wasn't.

"You need to eat a cheeseburger," he blurted out.

"Excuse me?"

"I'm just saying I could take you to The Bar and we could grab something to eat. They have some pretty decent food..."

"The Bar? The Bar has pretty decent food? I think I need to know your definition of *decent*."

He laughed. "Since Jack took over, trust me, things are better. You'll see."

I bit my bottom lip. "I'm not sure."

"Hey. You're back and I'm still here, and we can, well, you can let me figure out who you are, Brin. Say yes. Have dinner with me."

I blinked. Wait, did Garrett Pine just ask me out on a date?

"It's not a date or anything," he continued quickly. "I don't do that anymore. Burgers and reconnecting. That's it."

Right. Of course. I thought about telling him to go screw himself, but then I thought he was right. Dusty Creek was a small place. We were both living in it. If I had matured in the last five years, like I hoped I had, then our having a civil conversation wasn't the worst idea.

He was still technically my closest neighbor.

And the sheriff now. I had no plans to tell him about what had happened in LA or Dallas. Not when I knew how he would react. It would be casual.

"Okay."

"Good. I'll come out here and pick you up after my shift."

"Just tell me what time and I'll meet you there."

He frowned. "I can pick you up, Brin. Drop you off after on my way home."

"It's not a date, Garrett. I can meet you there."

I felt like he was about dig in, which would have made me dig in harder. Because the one thing he had to be absolutely certain of was that I no longer had any feelings for him whatsoever.

Even if I wasn't *totally* certain of that myself.

But I was done embarrassing myself in front of Garrett Pine.

"Okay. Around six work for you?"

I nodded.

"See you then."

He made his way back to his truck and I couldn't not watch him. No formal uniform now that he was the sheriff, just jeans and a chambray shirt with the Dusty Creek Sheriff's Department logo over the right pocket. But it was the way he moved. Something that told everyone around him that he held the power.

That he was the strongest, the fastest, the bravest.

Damn him for being hot. It made the not having a crush on him thing way more difficult.

Dinner. With. Garrett.

What could go wrong with that?

"Hey Garrett," I called out to him just as he was about to drive away. His window rolled down. "Congratulations on the promotion."

"It was an election," he called back. "But thanks."

Then I was waving and he was driving off.

Shit. Shit. Shit.

Great. I had already run but now I was rattled again because I was going to be having dinner, not a date, with Garrett Pine.

When it came to this level of stress there was only one thing to do...bake. Hate baking, where I created these masterful, sinful treats I could not eat. Feeling like I did today it was going to have to be...

"Cupcakes," I muttered to myself.

GARRETT

The Bar

This had been a mistake. I sat there sipping my beer, staring at the door like some puppy waiting for his master to come home, and realized I hadn't been honest with myself this morning.

I'd told myself I just wanted to find out whatever trouble Brin was having in LA.

That I still saw her as the girl I knew growing up.

That I hadn't been affected by the sight of her in shorts and a tank top with sweat dripping down her tanned, toned body.

Now my foot was tapping on the floor as the minute hand passed ten after six.

Ten minutes wasn't late. Ten minutes was in the window of normal.

Except when you had been a man who'd stood in the front of a church waiting for his bride to walk down the aisle.

Then ten minutes became ten years.

I was about to get up and leave. Maybe drive out to her place directly to tell her that standing me up had been a shitty thing to do. If she wanted to prove she'd matured, then this spiteful little stunt hadn't accomplished that.

The door to the bar opened and she walked in. She was wearing jeans, a pink silk shirt, and shoes so high I had no idea how she walked in them. But they made her legs look that much longer.

She sat across from me in the booth I had picked.

"Sorry I'm late. I couldn't find a parking spot on the street that was close. This place must be more popular than I remember."

Immediately all the tension I had been feeling left me. I had to unclench my hands from around my beer glass and stop my foot from bouncing. Remind myself that it was perfectly reasonable to be a few minutes late to a dinner meeting, not a date, because of parking.

"I told you—the food is decent."

Grace, who was a high school senior and worked the night shift, came over to take our order.

"I'll have a white wine," Brin told her.

"And two cheeseburgers with everything on them," I said.

"Actually, I'll just have a side salad." Brin smiled at the girl.

"What's the matter, you don't eat meat?" I asked.

She looked at me like I was insane. "Hello, I am a Texan. Of course I eat meat. I just can't eat cheeseburgers with everything on them."

"You need to eat a cheeseburger. Grace, bring us the burgers with her salad. We'll see if I can talk her into it."

"Yes, sheriff."

Brin waited until Grace left and then glared at me. "You keep telling me to eat cheeseburgers. If you have a point to make, why don't you just make it?"

"You're too thin. There, I said it." And immediately I realized I had no right to say anything about her body. But I had seen her in the shorts and tank top, and while she was super hot she still looked frail to me. Unprotected. Vulnerable.

"I am not! I'm TV thin and you're just not used to seeing that in the real world. Trust me, go to LA. You'll see it everywhere."

"TV thin," I snorted. "Translated—you don't eat enough to keep a rabbit alive. You need some substance in you. Something besides champagne."

She huffed. "See, there you go again. Making assumptions about me."

"How is that an assumption when I see you on TV?"

"You've watched my show?"

That seemed to startle her. As if it was unthinkable that I would. "My housekeeper likes to watch it. Sometimes it's just on the TV when I turn it on."

"Oh. Right. Anyway, what I do on TV is play a character."

"Hello? Correct me if I'm wrong, but I'm pretty sure it's a reality TV show. Emphasis on the word *reality*."

Brin shook her head. "You don't have a clue. The Cowboy Princess is a role. Of course I don't drink champagne all day. Of course I don't faint at the sight of flat shoes. Of course I don't shriek with horror at the discount shoe rack."

"I saw that episode. Shrieking was involved." I peeked under the table. "And those don't look like discount shoes."

She shifted, as if she was hiding her shoes from me. "Okay. Fair enough. But people have expectations about me I have to meet. Shoes being one of them. And also...sometimes I can't help myself."

She actually looked chagrined, which was adorable. "So you really won't eat a cheeseburger?"

"I learned that weight is power. And maybe now that I'm leaving the show I can eat one every now and then, but that doesn't mean I liked to be bullied into it."

"Fine. I concede to that. Wait, you're leaving the show? I thought it was popular."

She shrugged casually. "It is, but I'm ready to move on."

I leaned back in the booth, assessing her. She was deliberately not meeting my eyes.

"Because of this stalker? The one I saw on TMZ? I figured it was some story to create buzz for you and the show, but you reacted pretty strongly when I suggested as much yesterday."

"I don't really want to talk about it."

"Tell me."

Slowly she shook her head.

"I don't think..." She stopped talking when Grace came back with her wine. I watched as Brin smiled at the girl, which made Grace blush. Obviously Grace was aware of Dusty Creek's most famous citizen.

Brin waited until Grace left and then took a sip of her wine.

"It doesn't matter. It's nothing, really," she said with a shrug of her shoulder.

I couldn't tell if she was lying, and for some reason that bothered me.

"Then why did you come back? Dusty Creek must seem awfully small after spending years shuttling back and forth between Dallas and LA."

"Well, I don't know if you know, but Ronnie and Clayton are officially engaged again. And I'm planning their wedding. Not just any wedding. The wedding of the century! An event like that doesn't just plan itself. And Ronnie doesn't know this, but I'm also thinking of throwing another engagement party. Something to remove all the bad memories."

Yeah. Some pretty fucking bad memories.

"What you told me about that night was true, wasn't it?" I asked. Because I couldn't not. It was like running my tongue over a sore tooth. It only made the ache worse, but I couldn't seem to stop. "You saw them. Together."

My feelings for Betty had faded surprisingly quickly. Quickly enough that it made me question what I'd had with her. How could any of it have been real if she'd been lying the whole time?

But the betrayal, the lies, the abuse of trust. That had hit way harder. Much deeper.

"I'm sorry," Brin said. "I didn't mean to drag up bad memories."

I shook it off. "That's all she is, a memory. So, you're back for the wedding and then what?"

I had to change topics. She was looking at me. Like she used to when she was a kid. Like I could move the heavens and the earth. Like I was some type of invincible god when I was so far from that. It's just that there was something to be said for having Sabrina King believe in you.

"Then I don't know. Everything is on hold until after the wedding."

"And that's really the only reason you're home?"

She didn't reply, just nodded and sipped her wine. I didn't push the issue. It was fair to say, though, that I didn't think she trusted me completely. Probably with good reason.

Grace brought the food and I watched Brin stare down at the cheeseburger. Hard.

"American cheese, bacon, lettuce, tomato, and onion. Mayonnaise and lots of ketchup, too," I told her. "One bite. For me."

She smirked. "I don't owe you anything."

"Yes, you do. I made those bullies in the cafeteria stand down your freshman year. You totally owe me for that."

I watched her remove some of the bread from the bun and scrape off some of the mayonnaise. Then she cut the burger into quarters, picked one up, and bit into it. Her eyes nearly rolled back into her head.

"Fuck me, that's so good!" she groaned after she'd swallowed her first bite. "Oh, my God, I forgot what grease tasted like."

I wanted to tease her. I wanted to laugh at her. But I couldn't say a damn thing.

I had an immediate full-on erection. I was so stone hard that if she took another bite of that burger I was going to come in my jeans. Fortunately she set the remainder of the quarter down, wiped her fingers with a napkin, and took a fork to the salad.

"I don't know what's worse," she said, spearing a cherry tomato. "Not having it at all, or having a single bite so that you remember what you're missing."

I needed to think of something besides the expression on her face when she'd swallowed, so I focused on what she said earlier.

"What did you mean when you said weight was power?"

She arched her eyebrow like I was asking a stupid question. I suppose I was. Men assessed women by their appearance all the time. I knew that. But I think it was wrong to assume what was attractive to one man was the same for another.

"As a thin woman I had more power than as a fat one," she said baldly.

"You're saying only women of a certain size can be attractive? That seems rather harsh on your own sex."

She blinked. "No, absolutely not. Women are beautiful in every shape and size. And women who believe in themselves are attractive, no matter what other people think. But that wasn't the case for me growing up. I didn't set out to lose weight. I just started running because running helped me to cope with...all of it. The more I ran, the thinner I got. The thinner I got, the more power I had in my family. With my mother, with my father. Then, the thinner I got in LA, the more that made me a viable candidate for a reality TV show. The producers sought me out. Do you honestly think there would be a Cowboy Princess if I didn't look a certain way?"

I hated that she was right so I didn't reply.

"I should have clarified. Weight was about power for *me*. I recognize it's not the same for everyone. But this," she said casually, waving her hand over her face and body, "is all I have."

"You're more than how you look, Brin," I said, not happy with her self-assessment.

She tilted her head as if she was considering that. "Am I? Some people who watch *Cowboy Princess* wouldn't think so. At best, I'm known as shallow. At worst...I'm considered nothing more than a brainless Barbie doll."

"You said it yourself. You were playing a role."

"Hmm. Anyway, that's my life."

I watched her eyes dart to it. The quarter of the burger. Ketchup was running down the sides, a piece of bacon was sticking out. It was tempting as fuck, but she didn't stray from her lettuce.

"I can't imagine having that kind of willpower," I said suddenly, feeling guilty for having pushed it on her in the first place.

She shrugged. "I'm used to not getting what I want. It's easy."

That didn't make any sense. Sabrina was rich, beautiful. She could get anything she ever wanted.

"Sabrina, you have everything." I felt like I had to remind her of that.

She pushed away the burger and the half-eaten salad.

"No, Garrett," she said with a smile. "I have shoes."

And it damn near broke my heart.

7

SABRINA

One Week Later

"Hey, Jack," I called, even as I took a seat at the bar.

He lifted his chin at me and kept wiping down the beer glass in his hand. At this point he knew my wine of choice so I didn't bother asking for it. I wasn't sure it had been the best idea to come into town. The whole point was to lay low. But I was going a little stir crazy back at the ranch.

I had thrown myself into the wedding of the century, only to get ambushed by Clayton who'd insisted that it take place at the ranch with a mere one hundred and seventy-five guests. Huh. Those weren't even wedding of the *year* numbers.

I supposed it was what they wanted, so I had to defer. And I felt good about the state of things. After all, planning these types of events was my wheelhouse, so much so that I was running out of stuff to do, day in and day out.

I was still entertaining thoughts of throwing another engagement party. Given that that would be an even smaller event, I didn't see any problem pulling it off. I took out my phone, prepared to check out Pinterest for some party theme ideas, when I remembered I didn't have any accounts anymore.

Facebook, fine. Twitter, fine. Instagram had hurt, but I was coping. But losing Pinterest was killing me.

Jack delivered my wine and I thought about the small salad I would order. About how maybe, instead of doing balsamic and oil, I would get a little crazy with a light ranch dressing. Then I felt someone sit next to me.

I didn't have to turn my head. Didn't need him to say anything to me. Garrett was like a perpetual magnet in my life, one I was constantly drawn to.

"Brin," he said.

"Garrett," I said.

We had left our not-a-date on somewhat awkward terms. He had walked me to my car and I had gotten in before he could suggest anything. Like, can I give you a kiss on the cheek, or why don't we do this again, or I love you Sabrina and I always have.

It was important to avoid the traps.

I only looked back at him twice in the rearview mirror, which I considered pretty damn strong of me.

"I don't want you to think...I mean, I usually come here after my shift for a beer and dinner."

I did turn to him then. "I don't think anything, Garrett." Not that he purposefully sat next to me. Not that he wanted to talk to me, eat with me. See me. "Are you okay if I'm here?"

"Absolutely," he said. "You know...I really am glad to have you back. I mean it. We were...friends once. Right? A long time ago."

"Sure," I lied. I'd never thought of Garrett as anything so simple as a friend.

In front of Garrett, Jack put down a bowl of potato chips, like fresh homemade potato chips covered in salt so that you could see the white dots all over them. Then, next to that, he added a big bowl of what could only be sour cream and onion dip.

I gently brushed the corners of my mouth to make sure I wasn't salivating.

"Want one?" he asked. "Jack knows these are my weakness."

I glared at him.

"One chip, with a little dip. Not going to kill you, Brin." He was smiling, and then as if to torment me, he dug a chip through a healthy dose of dip and popped it into his mouth in one bite. I felt myself squirming on the stool. There, at the corner of his mouth, was some lingering dip. If I just leaned over and licked it off, surely it wouldn't be all that many calories.

Focus, Sabrina! This man does not and has never wanted you.

He was wiping his mouth. Boooo. Then he repeated the motion, only this time he held it out for me.

It was like Eve and the apple, only Garrett and a dip-covered potato chip.

I reached out to take it from his fingers, but he shook his head. "It will be too messy to transfer. Just open your mouth and I'll pop it in."

I glared at him again.

He smirked. "Okay, there was a little sexual innuendo in that statement, but I promise you it was unintentional."

I opened my mouth and he popped the chip in and it was everything that I remembered. Crispy, starchy, and creamy, all at once. Suddenly I realized I'd kept holding on to his hands long after I had chewed and swallowed it so I let him go.

When I opened my eyes he was staring at my mouth.

"You've got a little...cream at the corner there," he said roughly, pointing at my mouth.

I found a cocktail napkin on the bar and wiped the dip away.

"Better?" I asked.

"Depends on your definition." Again his voice was rougher than normal.

We both turned back to the face the bar rather than each other. I lifted my glass of wine and started drinking it in deep gulps. I noticed he was going after his beer pretty hard, as well. And his foot was bobbing up and down on the lower rung of his stool.

Oh, wait. Mine was, too. I finished my wine first and snapped the glass a little too hard onto the bar.

"Well, I've got to go. Been good seeing you, Garrett." I put another twenty down and thought how Jack was doing all right by me with tips.

"See you around, Brin."

He faced the bar and didn't look at me as I left. I only turned around once to look at him before I made it to the exit.

~

SABRINA

The King's Land—A Week Later

"I think I want to throw an engagement party for you and Clayton." I was sitting on my couch, phone to my ear, in my big, lonely ranch house and I realized I needed to do...something. Calling Ronnie seemed like a good idea.

Being back in Dusty Creek was both a blessing a curse.

A blessing that not a single weird thing had happened since I'd been back. No emails, no dead animals. Since I was completely off social media there were no messages to deal with there. I felt like I had finally given whoever had been chasing me the slip.

A curse though, too, because there wasn't a whole lot to do in Dusty Creek. There was one main street. One diner. One bar. One grocery store. Which meant any time I was out and about I was likely to run into the town's one sheriff.

Seeing Garrett wasn't good for my mental health. Seeing

Garrett when he was being nice to me…which was, like, ALL THE TIME now…was definitely messing with my head.

That night in the bar last week, well, I didn't even want to think about how I had practically sprinted to get away from him. Before I did something ridiculous like climb into his lap.

"No," Ronnie said instantly.

"No, this could be good. Get rid of all the old bad memories and replace them with good ones."

"No. It's enough that I've agreed to this massive wedding."

I snorted. "Hardly massive. You talked me out of what I wanted to do. Well, I should say, you got Clayton to lower the boom on me. A hundred and seventy-five people here at the ranch? That's like child's play. The food is done, the flowers are done, the invitations are out. The entertainment is pending, but that's just because I'm waiting for a contract. Did I mention the ice sculptures?"

"Ice sculptures? In June in Texas? For an outside wedding?"

I smiled. Now probably wasn't the time to tell her about the fireworks.

She sighed. "Sabrina, Clayton and I don't need any more exposure to the world. Besides, you know we're already married. An engagement party seems silly."

I suppose it did. Ronnie had dropped that bomb on me a few days ago. Apparently they were so in love they had both decided they didn't want to wait for the deadline to get married. When I asked Clayton why he'd done it, he just said he'd been waiting for five years and didn't want to wait any longer. The moment Ronnie told him she loved him, he'd taken them to a courthouse in Dallas to make it legal. He still wanted the big to-do, though. For Ronnie—and maybe himself, too.

"Fine. Maybe I'll just call it a party and be done with it. I'm me. People expect me to have fun parties all the time. This would be just one more."

"Tell me again why you need to throw a party."

"Because I'm bored!" I shouted and threw myself back on the couch. "I need something to do, and if you say shop, I'm never speaking to you again."

"Wedding planning is work."

I sat up. It wasn't enough to keep me occupied. To stop me from thinking about Garrett. And sour cream onion dip.

"I told you, most of it is already done. You and Bea need dresses. At some point I'll come to Dallas..."

"Oh, no. I'm not letting you bully me about dresses. I'll pick my own. Bea can pick her own, too."

Bea picking her own dress? This made me fractionally worried. "I did mention there is going to be press at this wedding, right? And cameras, lots and lots of cameras."

"I promise. I'll have a proper wedding dress. But we still don't need an engagement party."

"I need it," I groaned.

"You could get a job," Ronnie said gently.

"You're so funny," I quipped. "Me, working. Now that's the real joke."

"What about stuff around the ranch? We are more than oil and big energy industries. I believe The King's Land has a hundred and fifty head of cattle. Plus our stock-horse breeding program. Maybe start learning the family business."

"You mean go outside?" I asked incredulously. "In the dirt and mud with the animals? What shoes would I wear?"

"You mean they don't make Prada cowboy boots?"

I squinted my eyes. "Are you being for real right now? Because I could do some serious research."

"I have to go. Clayton's calling, but whatever you do...don't call it an engagement party. Too many bad memories!"

She hung up and I pouted. Didn't she get it? The point of replacing one engagement party with another was to erase all the bad memories. Like that night never happened.

The phone, still in my hand, started to ring again. I answered without even looking because I just assumed it was Ronnie calling me back, saying she forgot to tell me something.

"Yep," I answered. "What did you forget?"

There was a pause. As if she was surprised I had picked up so quickly.

"You can't run from me, Sabrina. I'll always find you. Soon we'll be together."

The strange dark voice echoed in my head and I dropped the phone like I had been holding a rattlesnake up to my ear.

I immediately reached for it and ended the call. Then I blocked the number.

I sat down on the couch and considered what had just happened. My hands were shaking and I shoved the phone between the cushions of the couch like that buffer might protect me from the person on the other end of the line.

I thought about the voice. It hadn't been *normal.* It was distorted, somehow. Something to disguise it so I wouldn't recognize it when I heard it in person. Why bother? Unless it was possible I knew this person? No, that couldn't be. There was a time I'd suspected people from the show, but nothing ever came of it.

But how did he keep getting my phone number? The last time I had changed numbers I hadn't really told Ronnie or Bea why. Only that a stupid fan had hacked my phone so I was taking precautions.

No biggie. Nothing to see here.

But if I changed my number twice in two months, they would definitely suspect something. Bea absolutely would call me on my bullshit. I couldn't think about that. For now the number was blocked and I would be super cautious about answering any calls.

But it meant he wasn't gone. I thought back to that day in Dallas, at the running trail. This was how I had felt then, certain I was being watched.

Was it just my phone or did he know where I lived? It wasn't like it would be hard information to find. I was the daughter of oil baron Hank King. The King's Land had been featured in multiple magazines. Yes, the ranch was isolated. With wide-open views in every direction. Not an easy place to sneak up on undetected.

Still, a girl had to take precautions.

I made my way back through the house to Hank's study. There was a gun safe in a corner of the room. I knew the combination, we'd all known the combination growing up. Hank was a believer in arming his girls for protection.

I pulled a nine millimeter Glock from one of the shelves. I would sleep with it under my pillow tonight and then think about what action I would take tomorrow.

My options seemed limited. I could wait it out, but I had done that these last few weeks by leaving LA and that hadn't worked. I could tell Garrett, let him know to be on alert, but everything in me cringed at having that conversation.

There was another option. An option that money provided. Money I wasn't certain I had yet, but maybe I could take the risk. I could hire a bodyguard. A professional who would come out to the house and stay here.

But for how long? Indefinitely?

Would this person ever give up? Or would it get worse?

Would it get dangerous?

GARRETT

Dusty Creek

I was coming out of the diner after lunch when I spotted her. Not that she was easy to miss, with her red leather jacket and four-inch high heels. Her long dark hair swinging down her back.

She was wearing the big round sunglasses again, and just like last time, I wanted to pull them off her face.

I shouldn't have followed her. In my gut I knew that. Sabrina King was part of my past, not part of my future. But she was crossing the street on her way to the grocery store, and suddenly I couldn't help myself.

I made my way down the sidewalk toward her. I told myself I had a bunch of reasons. I wanted to know why she'd bolted the other night when we were having drinks. I wanted to know if I had said or done anything to upset her. Had she been offended I had even offered her a potato chip?

Really, I think I just wanted to see her again. Make her smile.

I was coming up on her but I could tell she hadn't noticed me.

"Sabrina," I called to her. For a second she froze, and then she screamed. I saw her reach for her purse as she turned in my direction, and it was the craziest thing, but I felt like I needed to reach for my sidearm.

What the fuck?

As soon as she saw it was me, her body relaxed.

"Brin, what the hell?" I said as I approached her.

"You startled me." Her voice was a little raspy.

"In the middle of the day in front of the Piggly Wiggly?"

"So? I'm jumpy. Big deal." She had her arms crossed over her middle as if she was trying to protect herself.

Something didn't make sense, but I was starting to figure out that if I pushed her, her MO was to bolt.

I looked down at the purse she was clutching in her hand. "You carrying?"

Immediately her back went up. "I have a license. I'm allowed. Do you want to have a conversation about my Second Amendment rights? Do you?"

"Not particularly. I was just curious."

"Oh." Again her body seemed to relax. "Anyway, did you want something?"

I wanted to take her glasses off. I wanted to see her eyes. I wanted to know if she was really afraid of something or this was just Brin being Brin and putting on a show.

"No, I just needed to pick up some stuff for dinner. Now that spring is here I can grill again. I was thinking barbecued chicken. You should come over."

"Over where?"

"To my place. For dinner. When was the last time you saw the Pine ranch? Probably not since you were a kid."

She hesitated, but I kept walking toward the store and eventually she fell in step beside me. I picked a cart and started rolling it down the narrow aisles of Dusty Creek's lone grocery store.

Most folks did bulk shopping at the Costco two towns over. But the Piggly Wiggly served most of my needs.

Except they didn't sell condoms. The owner didn't believe in birth control, which was a pain in the ass. Buying condoms in bulk made me feel like more of a player than I was. And there was something depressing about seeing this massive box of unused condoms in my bathroom cabinet.

Wait. Why was I thinking about condoms?

Brin stayed mostly quiet until she started to pick up some fruits and vegetables and put them in my cart.

"I've never been to your ranch," she said quietly.

"Never? Huh, that seems crazy, but I guess all the big events happened at The King's Land."

"I guess."

"We can grill those peppers if you want," I suggested.

"I was buying them because I needed them for me. I suppose I should get my own cart."

"You can put them in mine. Just get extra, then."

She put them in the cart, then added a few of different colors. I didn't know why, but it made me happy to see our groceries comingled. Like I had won some kind of trust from her, in her allowing me to haul around her produce.

I picked up macaroni salad and potato salad. She picked up spinach and mushrooms.

"You need more vegetables in your diet," she grumbled when I reached for some coleslaw.

"You need more mayonnaise in yours."

She smirked at me and I felt like I had won again. The Sabrina who had walked into the grocery store had been distracted and tense. So tense that she'd screamed at just hearing her name.

Now she was herself and relaxed. We took our combined cart of food items and checked out what was hers and what was mine. Except when she reached for the peppers I stopped her.

"No, those are mine. Remember, I'm grilling them for us tonight."

She put a hand on her hip. "I don't even remember agreeing to have dinner with you."

"Sure you did. I said barbecued chicken, you said let's grill some peppers with that. I said let's add some potato salad...it's all right here," I said pointing to the counter of mixed food.

Once we had our groceries sorted and bagged, I walked her back to her car.

"What time can you come over?" I asked her.

"What time do you want me?"

Now, I thought. I wanted her now.

I shrugged. "I should be done my shift by six, so seven works."

She nodded and let me put her bags of groceries in the back of her sleek Mercedes. When that was handled, we stood there for a minute and I realized I couldn't let it go.

"Why are you carrying a gun, Brin? It's Dusty Creek. You know the crime rate here. If I make an arrest once a month that's a lot, and it's mostly Joe Kregger for getting drunk and disorderly again."

"I wanted to feel safe," she muttered. But the glasses, which she'd had perched on her head while we were shopping, were down now, over her eyes. I hated it.

"You don't feel safe in my town?" There was a little bit of pride on the line. I was the sheriff.

"I'm just taking precautions. There's nothing wrong with that."

No, there was nothing wrong with that. "Okay. I'll let you go and I'll see you tonight."

She nodded and stood back as she got into her car. Then I watched as she pulled away.

Something was going on there and I was going to find out what.

I was also going to have to do a lot of work to the get the grill ready for freaking barbecued chicken if she was going to believe I hadn't made all of that up on the fly.

Now who was pulling stunts?

8

SABRINA
Pine's Ranch

This is a mistake. I pulled my car up his long driveway and called myself a fool every inch of the way. Stupid, stupid, stupid, coming here for dinner. But what were my choices?

Sit at home with a gun in my lap while I hoped my phone didn't ring? Or spend the evening with a law enforcer where I would feel perfectly safe?

Except nothing was really safe with Garrett. Any time spent with him was a major effort in reminding myself that he was just being friendly. Neighborly. Curious.

While I could feel myself falling under the same Garrett Pine charm that had bewitched me my whole life. I was surprised when I pulled my car up next to his truck to find that he was actually outside waiting for me.

"Hey," I said as I got out of the car.

"Hey," he said tightly. "You're late."

I checked my watch. "You said seven."

"It's seven fifteen."

"Right. Because my hair didn't curl like it normally does, so I had to do it twice. But look. See? Now it's perfect."

I pulled a perfectly curled lock over my shoulder to show him.

He snorted. "I don't care how curly your hair is, Brin. Or what you look like, for that matter."

That's right, ladies and gentleman, the one man on the planet completely unmoved by my appearance. That's the guy I fell for.

"I know," I said, trying to be cheeky. "You prefer petite blondes."

"I prefer for people to show up when they say they're going to show up."

I was about to give him a hard time over fifteen minutes. Then I stopped.

"In fact, I wish you hadn't been so stubborn about letting me pick you up. I hate...waiting for people."

Right. Because he'd waited once and the person hadn't shown up. At all.

The fact that Betty had damaged a man like Garrett made me want to hunt her down and scratch her eyes out.

"Sorry I was late," I said. "I was just trying to look nice."

"You're fucking beautiful, Brin. You don't have to try so hard. Okay?"

It was like no other compliment I had ever received. Then he ran his eyes up and down what I had chosen to wear. A white denim flared skirt, a chambray shirt with the ends tied around my navel.

"Are those what I think they are?"

I smiled and stuck out my foot. "Cowboy boots. Real ones, too. I found an old pair in Bea's closet. Do not tell her we are the same shoe size. I won't have my collection being tainted by someone else's feet."

He laughed and the anger, or maybe it was something else, seemed to fade away.

"I believe I was promised barbecue."

"Yeah. Yes. Sorry. I didn't mean to jump down your throat."

I walked up to him and patted his cheek gently. "It's okay. I'm made of sterner stuff. I survived years of fat jokes, after all."

I breezed past him and boldly walked into the house. I waited for a dog to come barreling out of some room to greet me. I don't know why, but I always assumed Garrett was a dog type. A big, loveable, dopey dog seemed right up his alley.

But the house was quiet.

"This is the living room as you can see," he said, coming up behind me.

"No dog?"

The look he gave was confused. "How did you know about Champ?"

See? I knew Garrett. Sometimes I tried to tell myself it was all fantasy when it came to him. That I didn't really see him or know him as a person. But I did. It was bound to happen when you made someone the object of your obsession.

"Where is he?"

"Champ passed a few months ago. Right before your dad, actually."

"I'm sorry."

Garrett nodded. "Lived a good life. I basically grew up with him. I was giving myself some time to...I don't know, honor his memory, I guess. But I'm thinking I've got a puppy in my future pretty soon."

"Puppies!" I said, clapping my hands. "Mother never let us have any pets. She insisted it was because I was allergic, but I've never had a reaction to any animal I've ever been around. And there was this cat..."

The one that was killed because of me.

"You had a cat?"

"He wasn't really mine. He just let me feed him for a while. Anyway, I don't want to talk about that."

"Okay, well, let me show you outside. The house isn't much, but the one thing my dad did not scrimp on was the back deck."

I followed him through the living room and past the kitchen. Off the kitchen was a large sliding door that opened out onto a large brick patio. Garrett hadn't been kidding. There were a fireplace and a grill pit. A gas grill. Lots of sturdy furniture to hold up against a heavy Texas storm.

But the best part was the view. Land. Land as far as the eye could see. That was Texas.

"Have a seat and I'll get you something to drink."

I was about to sit down when I thought about what I had made this afternoon. "Oh! I left something in the car. Let me go get them and I'll be right back."

I made my way through the house and back out to the driveway. I opened the backseat door and pulled out the plate of cookies. I'd gone with chocolate chip because I thought Garrett looked like a chocolate chip kind of a guy. And since I had been right about him having a dog, I thought that was a good sign.

I came back in carrying my plate while he was pulling wine out of the refrigerator. I could see he had the chicken already coated with sauce and ready to be grilled. And he'd taken the macaroni salad and potato salad out of the containers and put them in bowls.

In other words, he'd made an effort. I was glad, then, to have taken the extra time with my hair, despite what he'd said, and glad, too, I was contributing something to this dinner.

"Cookies," I announced as I set the plate down on the counter.

His eyes lit up. "You made cookies?"

He obviously hadn't watched a lot of episodes of *Cowboy Princess*. Hate baking was a common event on the show.

"I did. Give them a try."

He pulled off the tinfoil I had used to cover them and took one. He bit into it and the groan he made was slightly sexual and smoking hot. On par with watching him eat a potato chip. I was used to people going crazy over my baked goods. It was part of the fun of hate baking. No, I couldn't eat it, but I loved watching other people's reactions. I wasn't, however, used to getting turned on by it.

Do not get aroused by him! Do not!

"Holy shit that's good."

I smiled. I couldn't help but be proud.

"It might possibly be my one skill," I said, a little cocky. "Well, that and shoes. And I love doing it."

"This might be the best freaking cookie I've ever had." He reached for another and handed it to me but I shook my head.

"Oh, no. I don't eat them. I just bake them and watch other people enjoy them. TV thin. Remember?"

"You don't eat them?" he asked, his voice a little rough.

"No. Sometimes if I'm messing with a new recipe I have to try a bite...you know, just to make sure I got it right. But once I have it down, then I just bake and enjoy the smells. My kitchen right now smells yum!"

He put the cookie down and turned away from me. I had this sense that he wanted to say something but he stopped himself.

"I got two kinds of white wine. I wasn't sure what you liked."

"A glass of that one," I said pointing to the bottle I recognized. "Just a little splash."

"Right, because you can't drink either."

Was he angry about that?

"Uh, hello, sheriff. I'm driving. I would think you might frown upon that."

He poured the glass and handed it to me. "You're two and half miles down a road that is deserted most of the time. I'll let a half of a glass of wine slip in this case."

"You're being awfully grumpy," I said as I sat on one the stools that butted up to a small kitchen island. His kitchen was about of quarter of the size of the one at The King's Land, but it oddly felt more comfortable. Homey. "Is it still because I was late or is it because you're just hungry in general?"

He snorted. "I am behaving a little like an ass, I suppose."

"Good thing this isn't a date," I told him. "Otherwise..." I made a motion with my finger indicating a slash and then a one.

"What the hell is that?"

"Wow. You really didn't watch my show a lot. That was my universal sign when I was on a date that I was subtracting points. I would find ways to do it subtly so that only the audience watching would realize what I was doing. They loved it. Didn't pull my chair out. Minus one. Didn't ask me any questions about myself. Minus one. Checked out another woman walking by. Minus one."

I showed him how I made the various different hand motions. A finger horizontal under my nose, then down my cheek. Against the wine glass, then sliding down the rim.

"I can't imagine guys lost a lot of points with that last one."

"You forget it was Los Angeles. Practically everyone is beautiful there."

"Sounds shallow," he grunted.

I took a sip of my wine. "Well, I'm shallow. So we fit."

He scowled at me again. "Are you trying to piss me off?"

I thought about that. "Not particularly."

"Geezus, Brin. You know what you are? You are fucked up. It's a good thing you came back to Dusty Creek. If for no other reason than to get your head on straight."

I blinked as his words hit home. "I'm pretty sure it was rude of you to say that to my face."

"Sorry," he barked. "But ever since you got back it's just been constant dumping on yourself. You're only what you look like. You having nothing but shoes. You're shallow. You can't eat because of whatever power struggle you're in, although you left the damn TV show that you said you were doing it for in the first place. You can't even eat what you obviously enjoy baking, but you light up like a fucking Christmas tree when you watch how I react to it."

"I...uh..." I didn't know what to say. I didn't know how to react. This was Garrett yelling at me for being *me.*

"What did I tell you all those years ago? When you were facing off against those sophomore assholes? Own your shit. It doesn't look like you listened to me at all. I mean, who the fuck raised you?"

"Hank and Jennifer raised me," I said, pushing off the counter and waiting until I knew my legs were steady and would hold me up.

"Right. Hank. Who wouldn't even stick up for his little girl when people were teasing you. That's why I stepped in at high school. I wasn't going to let that shit happen anymore, but maybe what I forgot was to show you how to fight back."

Fight back? Hadn't I transformed myself? Hadn't I gotten even with everyone who shit on me for being fat? I was the walking personification of fighting back. And he didn't get to take that from me.

"Fuck you, Garrett. How is that for fighting back? I'm sorry I can't be the woman you seem to think I should be. If only I had been...oh, I don't know, a virtuous blonde nurse then maybe that would have been better for you. Only I guess that didn't work out so well, after all!"

His face hardened then. "You've been waiting since you got back to get that shot in haven't you?"

I hadn't been. I didn't think I had been. I didn't want to hurt Garrett. I never wanted that. As many times as he'd hurt me.

I could feel my lips wobble and I knew I needed to leave. I practically sprinted for the front door. I threw it open and raced to my car. I hadn't brought a purse or anything. Just the cookies.

The fucking cookies I made for Garrett.

So I had left the key fob in the center console. I fumbled with it to get the car to start, although I wasn't sure why I was in a hurry. Because it wasn't like Garrett was storming after me.

Why would he?

9

GARRETT

Pine's Ranch

Shit. What the fuck just happened? I tried to think. She'd been late, which made me crazy. She wore cowboy boots and made me chocolate chip cookies, which also made me crazy. I'd come down on her like a ton of bricks for being too damn hard on herself. And she'd fired back with the one weapon she had.

It was a good one, too. Because the whole time during my engagement, she had known what Betty was. A cheater. She'd told me to my face, expecting me to believe her and I hadn't. She must have laughed her ass off when she heard what Betty did to me at the church.

I stopped then and ran a hand through my hair. No, she wouldn't have laughed. She would have felt bad for me. Sad, even.

She's not good enough for you.

That's what Brin had always told me about the women in my

life. It sort of sucked to know she was right. I looked around my empty home and thought of the things I was missing.

I'd thought I would have long been married by now, maybe already had a couple of kids. It's what Betty had told me she wanted. And she had, she just hadn't wanted those things with me.

So, fine, I gave up on all that crap. Who needed it?

Then why were you freaking out that Brin was fifteen minutes late?

Shit.

Because I'd been anxious to see her. Anxious to cook for her and just talk with her. Staring at the clock, wondering if she had changed her mind, twisted my guts up. I didn't want this woman to change her mind about me.

Maybe that was my problem. I had lived in the world for a long time, confident that Sabrina King of The Kings had a crush on me. I wanted that back. The idea of knowing someone in my life would put me first, above anyone else.

It was nice. It also made me a raging asshole.

I needed to apologize. I looked around for my keys and found them on the table by the front door. I jogged out to my truck, trying to think of what the hell was I going to say.

I was still running through it when I pulled up to her gate. Damn, the gate. I didn't want to buzz her and give her the chance to tell me to go away. Instead, I left the truck at the bottom of the drive and hopped the low fence onto the property. The gate kept unwanted vehicles out, but that was about it.

I marched up the driveway and got to her front door. I pounded on it because it felt good. Loud and hard, and as upset as I was it gave me a little relief.

Except I heard a scream, a loud scared one from inside the house. Damn it. "Sabrina!" I shouted. "Sabrina! Answer me."

I reached for the knob and jerked on it, but there was no way I was getting past the large wooden door.

But I knew from experience the back kitchen door off the sunporch was pretty flimsy. I jogged around the expansive mansion until I saw the kitchen door. The lock on this door was just a latch hook that I bulled my way through. Once inside, I started running through the house. That scream. That hadn't been about anger or outrage.

It had been about fear.

"Sabrina! Where the hell are you?"

Turning the corner out of the hallway, making my toward the living room, I saw her sitting on the floor with her back to the wall. There was a gun in her hand but she wasn't aiming it. She was crying.

No. Sobbing.

Cautiously, because a sobbing woman with a gun in her hand was not something to take lightly, I approached her. "Brin," I said softly.

Her body jerked but she still didn't look at me.

I crouched down beside her and took the gun out of her hand. "Brin, talk to me."

She shook her head.

"Where are Ronnie and Bea? Hell, where is Trudy?"

She shook her head again.

"I can't help you if you won't talk to me."

She looked at me then, and I could see it, the bone-deep fear in her eyes. "You won't believe me."

"Okay, let's start with the easy stuff. Ronnie and Bea?"

"Ronnie's back in Dallas and I think Bea went back to Austin."

"Oscar and Trudy?"

She sniffed. "They're on an extended cruise."

"Who's taking care of the horses?"

"Walt's son comes over every day."

I nodded. "So, with Ronnie back in Dallas you're out here by yourself most of the time."

She nodded.

Okay. That made some sense. Big sprawling house, all alone. Someone pounding on the door. "Did I scare you? Pounding on the door that way."

She nodded tightly.

"Honey, I'm sorry. I didn't mean to. I was just trying to be loud enough so that you would hear me."

She swallowed and rubbed her nose against the sleeve of her shirt. "It's not that. I...I don't want to talk about it."

I stood then and reached my hand out to her. "Sorry again, but I don't hear you scream like that, find you curled up on the floor with a gun in your hand, and let you get away with not talking about it."

"Why are you even here?" she asked even as she took my hand and let me pull her to her feet. "You hate me, remember?"

And that was about the farthest thing from the truth I had ever heard.

"I was here to apologize, but now I'm here on official business." I directed her over to one of the long leather sectionals in what I believed was the game room. A more manly space, as opposed to all the delicate furniture in the living room. I sat down and pulled her down next to me.

She didn't resist, but she still wasn't looking at me.

"Talk, Brin. Why were you freaking out just then? Why are you walking around Dusty Creek with a gun?"

"Why didn't you buzz at the gate?" she fired back. "Then I would have known you were coming."

"I didn't want to give you the chance to blow me off. I wanted to talk to you. Apologize. Maybe try to explain some stuff."

"You don't have to," she mumbled. "I know why you were mad. I shouldn't have been late just to fix my hair. That was a stupid reason and it's disrespectful to be late."

"But your curls *were* perfect," I teased. She let out a huff of laughter.

I bumped my shoulder against her and then, because I liked

it, liked the feeling of her pressed against me, I stayed there. She didn't move away so I assume she liked it, too.

"Okay, now talk to me, to Sheriff Pine. What has you so spooked?"

She stood then, and I thought it was going to be another trick to avoid answering me. Instead she brought back her cell phone. She put her thumb on it to open it and then she showed me what was on the screen.

It was a picture of her. From today. In the red leather jacket. Making her way across the parking lot of the Piggly Wiggly.

"Someone sent you a picture of you? A fan?"

"I don't think so," she said softly. "I think it was him."

"Ex-boyfriend?" Because that would have made sense. Someone who'd had Brin and didn't want to let her go.

She shook her head but said nothing else.

"Brin," I growled, suddenly desperate for the answer.

"I don't want to tell you," she insisted. "You'll think..."

"I'm not going to think anything," I snapped at her. "I'm going to believe what you tell me. Now tell me who the fuck took this picture of you."

She jerked again and I realize it probably wasn't fair. She'd been afraid since she got the picture. Afraid when someone was suddenly banging on her door. Now I was trying to bully her. But I needed answers if I was going to help her.

"Is that how you interrogate all your victims, sheriff?"

I stood then, so I would tower over her. Brin was tall, but at six-two I forced her to look up at me.

"I do what it takes to get answers."

She crossed her arms around her middle and sat back down on the couch. "I want you to know you have been a total jerk tonight. And I made you cookies."

"So noted," I said, sitting down next to her, facing her. "Now talk."

"Remember the stalker? The one you thought my publicist

hired to create buzz for me. Yeah, well, my publicist, which I don't have, by the way, didn't hire the stalker. He's real. Now you can say how it's all made up for TV and that I'm just pulling a stunt and go along your merry way. I know what I'm going to do."

"I saw you sobbing on the floor, Brin. I heard you scream. I don't think you're pulling a stunt."

"You didn't think the stalker was real."

"No," I admitted. "I saw a banner on entertainment news. I thought it was made-up horseshit. You're telling me now it isn't, so I'm listening. How did it start?"

"He's been around since the show started. Emails. To the show's website originally. It was pretty standard stuff. I love you, Sabrina. I want to make you mine. I didn't think much of it. It wasn't too out of line from the normal fan mail. But then it started coming to my personal email and it freaked me out. I would close the account and open another, only to have that account hacked. Nothing then that really scared me, but in these last few months something has changed. He hacked my social media, which I had to shut down. Then the emails became more lurid. More intense about what he was going do to me. Then it was phone calls. Then...the cat. This feral cat that lived behind my house in the hills. It was killed. Put on my doorstep for me to find. It wasn't like a pet or anything. I did leave it dry food... Anyway, that was it. I wanted to be done with the show, anyway. This just made that decision simpler."

"Except he sent this picture to your phone."

She nodded. "Which means he was in town. Plus he called me the other day on my new number. I have to change my number again. Ronnie and Bea are going to know something bad is up, and Ronnie doesn't need this with everything she has going on."

She stood again and started to pace.

"That's why you're carrying?"

"Do you blame me?"

"You know how to shoot?" I asked her.

She rolled her eyes at me. "My father was Hank King. I think it might be the only thing he taught us. That and we weren't sons."

I nodded. "Fine, you know how to shoot, but would you shoot?"

She seemed less certain about that. "I don't know. But like I said, it doesn't matter. When I saw the picture... He's here and I need a plan."

"You keep saying *he*," I said, jumping on her certainty. "Are you sure of that? Do you think you've seen him?"

She nodded. "I think so. I was in Dallas. On a jogging trail. There was a guy in a hoodie and it looked like he was watching me. When I took off I could have sworn he started to chase me. I ran to other people to get help but when I turned around he was gone. I could have been paranoid. I don't know anymore. Maybe I *am* making this all up."

I didn't see paranoia, I saw escalation. Emails, calls, threats, and finally confrontation. The picture was a warning. Letting her know he was close.

"What did he say on the call?"

"The voice was distorted. But he said that I couldn't run away and that soon we would be together."

"Is that what you're doing back in Dusty Creek? Running away?"

She fell back down onto the couch. "I guess. I'm also trying to figure my life out. I didn't want to do the show anymore. I knew that. It's a risk, but I have enough savings that I thought it was worth it to take a step back and think about what I wanted for my future."

That didn't make sense. What risk? Sabrina was a King. "You keep saying that, about the money and the show. Like you had to work."

"Uh, yeah. You think Hank was going to fund my life in LA?

Hell, no. He had a condo there and even that was off-limits. He was as pissed at me for leaving as he was at everyone else. Why do you think he left everything to Clayton? Oh. I guess you didn't know that."

I shook my head and cursed softly under my breath. "Hank didn't leave his children this ranch, his fortune?"

She snorted. "Oh, he left it to his child. His male child."

"Dylan." I had only met Dylan one time. He'd come out to the ranch for a summer, and there had been a Fourth of July blowout my family and I had attended. I knew his story, but I didn't really know Dylan. Which I suppose pretty much summed up his family's relationship with him. Dylan was like ether. There was always a whiff of him around but you never actually saw him.

"Dylan has until the wedding to come home to claim King Industries. If he doesn't, then it all goes to Clayton. It's a lot of money to walk away from but we all believe Dylan is never coming back. If he doesn't, Clayton inherits everything."

This time I stood. Too irritated to sit. "Fuck me. Hank really was an old bastard wasn't he? It wouldn't have occurred to me he wouldn't have protected you. So all that time in LA, you were on your own?"

She shrugged. "It wasn't like I worked the streets, Garrett. Relax. I had rich friends who put me up. I had tons of clothes and jewelry I could pawn. And I was Sabrina King. If I walked into a store and tried on something that made me look fabulous, nine times out of ten they would just let me have the clothes as long as I said where they came from. I was a walking advertisement. When I got the show that only increased. I guess I didn't think of that when I walked away. Now I'll have to buy my Choos at retail price!"

"Can we focus on what's important?" I snapped.

She pouted. "You mean on the guy who *wants me to be his*. I would rather not."

"Stop pretending, Brin. You're scared. Legitimately."

"I am. But I told you I have a plan."

"And what's that?"

"I'm going to hire a bodyguard. Somebody who knows how to shoot and *will* shoot. It's the only way I'll feel safe."

I didn't like it. The idea of some store-bought cop with hulking muscles and a big gun looming around her all the time.

Why? Why didn't I like that?

I didn't think on it too hard. I just rolled with what my gut was telling me. And it was saying that there was a better way to protect Brin.

"I'll do it."

"You'll do what? Find me a bodyguard?"

"Better. I plan to *be* your bodyguard."

10

SABRINA

Pine's Ranch

"I don't think this is such a good idea." I put the bag he'd made me pack down in the foyer and wondered for the thousandth time how he had talked me into coming back to his ranch with him.

"What do you mean? It's a perfect idea. You need protection and I'm the sheriff."

"Last time I checked you were responsible for all the citizens of Dusty Creek but I don't seem them camped out in your living room."

"Yeah, well, no one other than you is under an immediate threat. Besides, you're a target at The King's Land. Everyone knows who you are and where the ranch is. Now he has no clue where you are and that's to your advantage. You let everyone in town think you're still at the ranch and this can work. Tell me again the timeline of events. When did it become scary?"

"I told you I had been getting emails for as long as the show has been on, but it feels like it was after Hank's funeral that things just seemed to go from weird to crazy to super intense. I came home and we found out about the will from his attorney, Madison. Then everything blew up between Ronnie and Clayton..."

"Wait," he said, coming to a pretty obvious conclusion about their upcoming wedding. "Is Ronnie only marrying him because she has to? Because that's not right. There has to be a better way. Contest the will. Something."

I shook my head, trying to understand what Ronnie was thinking. "Honestly, I didn't understand why she was doing it at first. Probably for Bea, maybe me, too. But the crazy part about it was that they had never stopped loving each other. Now they're together and really happy."

"How is that for irony?"

"I know. Right. But back to your original question, that's when it got scary. After the funeral."

He seemed to think about that for a second and nodded. "It makes sense that Hank's death might have triggered this person to act. It was national news. He would know it happened and would see you as being more vulnerable now."

That was almost funny. "More irony. They wouldn't know how unprotective of his daughters Hank actually was."

I made my way back inside to the kitchen. All of the food he'd been planning to serve was still out. I realized two things. I was hungry and there was a reason I had left in the first place.

"I can fire up the grill. There's still time to save dinner."

He came up behind me and then around to the refrigerator. "You can put your stuff away if you like. Down the hall, last door to your right. It's my old room and I haven't had a chance to turn it into a proper guest room, so ignore all the trophies and stuff."

Right. Because Garrett wanted me to sleep in his room tonight. "Not good."

He poked his head out of the fridge and was now holding a plate of chicken he'd prepared for grilling. "Did you say something?"

I shook my head. Instead I went back to get my bag and then I made my way past the kitchen down the hall that led to the bedrooms. The Pine family home was a sprawling ranch with an old Spanish hacienda feel to it. I also knew he raised rodeo bulls and had a stable out back with two horses.

I opened the door and stepped inside a teenage boy's room. His dresser was covered in the various athletic trophies he'd won. There were ribbons and school certificates, too.

Maybe it had been easy for him. After all, Dusty Creek High School had probably only had five hundred students total. It's why Jennifer had wanted to send me to private school. She felt my education would be lacking if I went to a local school.

I, however, had been determined to go for at least one year where Garrett had been going. It was one of the few battles I won with Jennifer because Hank didn't concern himself all that much with a girl's education.

Now here I was. In the place I always wanted to be. Only not an hour ago he'd basically listed all the many ways he didn't like me.

I inhaled and thought I could still smell him. High School Garrett. Protector Garrett. It was my most favorite smell ever. I was less certain about Bodyguard Garrett.

I made my way back down the hall taking in all of the family pictures hanging on the walls. Garrett was an only child and his parents had been a little older when they had him, so all the photos were of him at various stages of life. Baby, toddler, teenager.

I stopped in front of the picture where he was on one knee in his high school football uniform.

That Garrett made me feel awesome.

Today's version made me feel…cautious.

When I got back to the kitchen I could see the sliding glass door was open and Garrett was laying out chicken on the grill. I could also see he'd poured me a new glass of wine.

"Not going anywhere now, I suppose." I took a healthy sip from the glass.

"Okay," he said, coming back inside. "Another thirty minutes and we should be good."

I nodded.

"It will almost be like I didn't jump down your throat earlier."

"It's okay. I get it."

"No, I'm pretty sure you don't. Look, Brin, I wasn't trying to call you out for anything other than being too hard on yourself. I think you've got it in your head that you have to be this perfect version of Sabrina King or no one will want you around. That simply isn't true."

I had evidence to the contrary but I wasn't going to point that out.

"How does this work?" I asked him instead.

"How does what work?"

"You being my bodyguard. Am I just supposed to stay here all day? And how long does that last? I need a way to end this."

"The only way that happens is if we catch him or he loses interest."

"There won't be any new episodes of *Cowboy Princess* but I'll be in reruns forever."

"So we catch him. You said he approached you in Dallas. If he did it once, he'll try it again. When he does I'll be there."

"You make it sound so easy."

"It won't be. But from everything you've told me, he's escalating. Especially if he chose to follow you to Dusty Creek. You were right to put Jack on alert. I'll make sure everyone around here knows to be on the lookout for any strangers. And I'll have my deputies do drive-bys at The King's Land when they can. I'll need the code for the gate."

I nodded.

"You should have told me, Brin. That first night at the bar, when you left, that's what you meant about wanting me to believe you."

I shrugged. "I didn't think you would."

"What happened was five years ago," Garrett said, not looking at me. "You could have given me a little credit for getting over it."

"What happened was an hour ago," I countered, reminding him of our fight.

He sighed. "Fair enough. You can always go, Brin. Stick to your original plan and hire someone."

"It would be simpler." Simpler. But, if I was being honest with myself, I didn't think I would feel any safer than I did right now.

He nodded even as he approached me. "Yeah. It would be. A lot. Because I bet the person you hired wouldn't have spent all day thinking about how he wants to kiss you."

Gulp. "Did you just say that?"

"Yeah, Brin. I just said that. Now, how about we eat some fucking chicken. Okay?"

GARRETT

"Shouldn't we talk about the kissing thing?" Brin asked, even as she picked apart the chicken breast with her fingers. I'd given her three pieces, at which she'd rolled her eyes, but at least she was on to her second piece.

That pleased me. Feeding her pleased me. Having her here when I knew there was danger for her outside...pleased me.

"No," I said, taking a slug of my beer. I didn't know why I had told her. I just knew it was the reason I had jumped all over her earlier this evening. She made me wait. I'd been waiting for her, and when I considered why I had been so damn anxious it was because I knew I wanted her.

"But *you* said it."

"I said it because I meant it. Hiring someone might be easier and better for both us." Even if the idea made me cringe. Because now I could admit that the reason I didn't like the idea of someone protecting her was because I wanted to do it.

"Is that what you want?"

"No," I said. "I don't. I want to do it. I want to protect you. Why? Because, let's face it Brin, throughout your life I've done it the best. From bullies, from your father, your mother. Then you go off to LA and the next thing I know someone is stalking you."

"You say it like it's my fault!"

I did. Because all of it was her fault. Making me feel like I was about to jump out of my skin when she was around. Making me want to kiss her. Making me want to tear apart anyone who would even consider laying a hand on Sabrina King.

Sabrina King was *mine*. She had been since she was eleven years old and was so damn enamored of me she could barely speak whenever she saw me.

Which was the problem. Because I didn't want a woman again. Not in a serious way. I didn't want all that came with it. To be with someone like that...there needed to be trust. I flat-out didn't have it to give anymore.

"Your staying here makes sense. He won't know to look for you here. A bodyguard wouldn't give you that. Unless he took you to some remote place and locked you up for a while."

"I didn't want to do that," she said even as she sucked barbecue sauce off a finger. An act that wasn't helping the whole I-can't-kiss-her thing. "I wanted to come home. Help Ronnie with the wedding."

"Then you stay here," I said, taking another sip of beer.

"Everyone else thinks you're at The King's Land. You need to come into town, you find me first and I'll set you up with a detail. Either myself or a deputy."

"Even though you want to kiss me."

"Yes. Even though. Because here is the thing, Brin. I won't."

"Oh."

Was that disappointment? Did she look disappointed?

"Because you don't like me," she assumed. "Not really."

"Wrong. Because I do like you. But I don't want to like another woman again. Not one I'm fucking."

She scrunched up her nose. "So you're never *with* women?"

I laughed, shaking my head. "I fuck women, Brin. I fuck them and forget them. I obviously can't do that with you. And since kissing you is only going to make me want to fuck you, no kissing. Get it?"

"How do you even know I want to kiss you?" she asked, flipping her hair back over her shoulder. Then she did that thing with her finger...the minus one.

I stood up from the deck chair where I was sitting and walked over to hers. I braced my hands on the armrests so she was essentially trapped. She looked up at me with those wide brown eyes. So dark, so filled with emotion all the time. It's why I hated it when she wore sunglasses. I could see everything inside Brin as long as I could see her eyes.

I leaned and whispered into her ear. "You've wanted to kiss me for a very long time, Sabrina King. Are you saying now, after a mere five years, you no longer want that?"

I could hear the rush of her breath. I could see the way her pulse was beating in her neck. And when I pulled back it was there in her eyes. That look that made me, lowly Garrett Pine, a god.

"Maybe?"

I leaned down and took her mouth. It was a mistake. I knew it because it felt too damn good. Soft lips. She tasted like wine and barbecue sauce. When I pushed my tongue between her lips she gasped and the next thing I knew, her hands were in my hair. Like she couldn't stop herself from touching me. Opening herself to me.

Slowly I pulled away. Then I straightened. "Yeah, I was right. Kissing you only makes me want to fuck you. So no more of that."

She sighed and slumped a little in her chair. "You're probably right. Kissing leads to sex and the truth is...well, the honest truth is I hate sex."

It was like a punch to the solar plexus. And I was pretty sure it sealed my fate. Because there was no way in hell I wasn't now bound and determined to make Sabrina King not hate sex.

"Why do you hate sex?" Which was probably the worst question to ask someone when you were trying to avoid the topic.

"I know everybody says it's the greatest thing. But I think all those romance novels I read as a teenager were total horseshit. At best it's been uncomfortable, and at worst it has really hurt."

It was like I could feel the red haze of fury over take my eyes. "Someone hurt you during sex?"

"Only with his penis," she said, like that didn't count. "I had this idea that I might be gay. And the producers on the show thought that would be awesome for ratings. They did this whole set-up for me to kiss a woman for the first time, and I realized that I wasn't into that, either. I mean, I'm pretty sure you should be attracted to the same sex if you're gay."

"I'm pretty sure that's how it works," I muttered. Naturally, I still wanted to know the asshole who had hurt her with this penis so I could rip it the fuck off his body.

Except Brin stood and started clearing our plates to take them back to the kitchen. I moved to get the sliding glass door for her, still at a loss as to what to say.

She stopped and smiled. "You were right. I did always want to kiss you. I'm glad I got to. Even if it was just once." She pecked me on the cheek and breezed back inside.

I watched her scrape plates and load the dishwasher like she hadn't just altered my life irrevocably.

11

SABRINA

A Few Days Later

"You want me to do what?" I asked him as we stood in the barn where he kept his two horses, Evelyn and Nora. I had recently been introduced. "Have you met me?"

"You said you were bored," he pointed out.

"I was looking for creative suggestions not actual work."

"Stables have to be mucked."

"Yes, by mucking-type people. I'm a Cowboy Princess!" I screeched.

He smirked and handed me the shovel. "Not anymore. Now you're just a regular old girl from Dusty Creek. A little hard work might help you through that transition."

"I didn't know this whole bodyguard thing came at the cost of slave labor," I mumbled.

"You said you wanted to stay here on the ranch."

I had. Not because watching Garrett work would necessarily

be boring, but I didn't want everyone in town to know what was happening. The rule was that when I was in town, either he or a deputy would follow me. People would see that and start speculating.

"What am I supposed to do about shoes?"

Garrett looked at my feet. "You're wearing cowboy boots."

"Yes, but they are the only ranch-type shoes I have. I don't want to get horse poop on them."

"It's horse shit. And fine." He left me and went to open a trunk that sat just inside the door of the stables. "I'm pretty sure my mom...yeah, here they are."

He pulled out two long black rubber hideous-looking things.

I screeched. "What are those?

He laughed. "I thought only your character on TV squealed at ugly shoes."

"Don't call those rubber abominations shoes!"

"Fine. I'll call them what they are. Galoshes. You can wear these while you're cleaning out the stalls. And once that's done you've got to pitch them some clean hay. Evelyn and Nora are counting on you."

"They're in for some disappointment," I warned.

"You don't have to do this," he laughed. "You said you wanted something to do and these are just some of the chores I have to take care of."

I took the shovel from him and gasped at how heavy it was.

That only made him laugh harder. I snarled but he didn't seem intimidated.

"Fine. I'll do it. Just so I feel like I'm pulling some of my weight around here."

"Whatever, Brin. You have my number. You hear or see anything, you call me. But since no one knows you're here but me, you should be perfectly safe."

I nodded. It was odd but I felt safe. Garrett wasn't going to let anything happen to me. He was right about that. He'd always done a bang-up job being my hero. I set the shovel aside and followed him out of the barn and back to his driveway.

He got in his truck and gave me a wave, and I waved back at him thinking how domestic it all felt. I'd been sleeping here the last few nights. In his bed—granted, his *old* bed—my head on the pillow he used to sleep on. And now I was sending him off to work and I would be here when he came home.

I should bake him something. Something way better than just plain chocolate chip cookies. There were my chocolate pudding cookies. If I gave him those he might kiss me again.

Did I want that?

No, I told myself logically. He said he didn't want a relationship and I had no interest in fucking for fuck's sake.

Maybe Garrett would be different.

No, I told myself. That was wishful thinking. That was the fourteen-year-old girl still inside me who thought that we were going to be together forever. Then we weren't. Then real life happened and I learned the hard way that kisses don't always lead to mind-blowing sex and Garrett was just a crush I had to get over.

No, not get over, *was* over. I was totally over, one hundred percent over him.

Then why are you thinking about kissing him again?

"Because I'm a fool," I said to no one. Shaking off all my thoughts about Garrett, away I went to do something practical, like clean up horseshit.

Stalls mucked, fresh hay put down—I think Evelyn and Nora were pretty happy with me. There was sweating...so gross. But it felt real, which I didn't mind. Unlike sweating because the lights we needed to film were too hot. I was just stepping out of the foul galoshes and back into my cowboy boots when I heard a faint mewling sound.

I looked around the barn and followed the sound to where it was coming from, seriously hoping I wasn't about to find some big rat or something. Then I saw it, a little bundle of fur in the corner of the barn, all alone.

I ran to it and saw that it was a kitten. So tiny, and it was crying.

"Where's your mother, honey?" I crooned to it even as I brought it to my chest. "Did she forget you?"

More cries as I looked around, waiting to see if the mother was anywhere in sight. But there was no cat and no other kittens that could see. I couldn't leave the poor thing. What if his mother never came back for her baby?

I lifted the black-and-white ball of fur up to my face.

It cried again and I imagined it was hungry. It was so small it couldn't have been weaned yet. I didn't have a clue what to do. I took it back up to the house and found some milk and a flat dish. I poured some milk in the dish and set the kitten down, but it was as if he wasn't sure what to do with it, either.

Or maybe he didn't have the strength. I dipped my pinky into the milk and dripped it into the kitten's mouth. That seemed to work, so I kept doing that until eventually the kitten dozed off.

Cradling it against my chest I knew I was down for the count. This poor creature needed my help and I was going to save it. First things first—I needed a vet to check him out.

I took a throw blanket I found in the closet and used that on the front seat of the car to form a little nest for it. Then, driving as slow as I could, I made my way into town. Dusty Creek only had one vet, who handled small and large animals, but I knew Charlotte from high school was now working as Doc's assistant. She would help me out in an emergency.

I parked in front of the Doc's office and got out. I looked down the street and could see the police station, Garrett's truck parked out front. I thought about telling him I was here, but I didn't think this would take long. I would have Charlotte check out my kitten, pop down to the Piggly Wiggly to get some supplies, and be back on the ranch before he knew it.

"Sound like a plan?" I asked my new friend. Except my new friend was still sleeping.

I gathered the blanket up and headed inside the office.

"Well, it definitely must have been abandoned," Charlotte said as she checked the animal out. She was a few years older than me and had gotten her license only recently, but she seemed to know what she was doing. "It happens. Mother starts to move the kittens and maybe something happens to her or she forgets how many she had."

"That's terrible. Can I save it? Or is it too young?"

Charlotte opened a cabinet and came back with a tiny syringe with a rubber tip. "It will be work. But if you nurse him and he takes the nipple, you might be able to save him. Small amounts every two hours until he gets his strength up. Then in a week or two you can try him on wet food. I can send you home with some formula."

I nodded. "I can do it. I can feed him. It's a boy?"

"It's a boy. And if you do plan to keep him, make sure you bring him back in a few weeks to have him neutered and vaccinated."

"I'll do it. Thanks for this, Charlotte," I said, smiling as I lifted up my kitten. "I'm going to be your momma now, baby."

It cried again, and maybe it was wishful thinking but I thought he sounded a little stronger already.

"I'm going to name you Romeo, because you stole my heart." I brought his tiny body back into the cradle of my chest.

"Thought Sheriff Pine already did that," Charlotte laughed.

Instinctively, I stiffened. "What do you mean?"

"Saw you two together at The Bar a couple of nights ago. Figure now that you're back and he's single...well, everyone in Dusty Creek knew Sabrina King was gone over Garrett Pine."

"Not anymore," I said quickly. "We're just...friends. He's helping me out with something. That's all."

Charlotte looked at me and I could feel my cheeks heating up. Friends probably didn't kiss the way we had. But that had been a one-time thing. Garrett said it himself. It didn't matter if I was thinking about doing it again if he wasn't thinking about doing it again.

"Friends," Charlotte said with a ton of innuendo. "Okay."

"We are," I insisted. "Now, tell me what I need to get for Romeo."

I left Charlotte's office with an armload of formula and some extra nipples. Next it was off to the grocery store. I wasn't sure how Mr. Dawson, who owned the Piggly Wiggly, would feel about my bringing an animal into the store but I wasn't about to leave Romeo by himself.

Instead, I emptied my purse and tucked Romeo inside my Kate Spade bag.

"Try not to pee in there, buddy."

But Romeo seemed to content to snuggle down. With my wallet in my hand, I breezed through the store, picking up a litter box and sand. And some toys he probably wasn't strong enough to play with yet, but I couldn't have a baby kitten and not have some toys for him to play with.

I probably went a little overboard, but I was a new mother so it was okay.

I rolled my cart to my car, loaded the supplies into the trunk, and was about to get into the car when I stopped. I couldn't say what it was. A feeling. An intuition. I just knew, knew someone was watching me.

I thought about the gun I had left at Garrett's place. I had been so focused on getting help for Romeo it hadn't even occurred to me to bring it with me. Slowly I turned around, hoping that I was just being paranoid.

It was him. The guy with the hoodie from the jogging trail. The hood this time pulled low over his face. He was also wearing sunglasses.

And he was staring right at me.

This time he didn't run after me. Instead, he just pointed directly at me.

I wasn't crazy. It was him. I screamed and started to run, holding my purse and Romeo close to my chest.

Garrett. I needed to get to Garrett. Garrett needed to see him. See that he was real.

I sprinted for the police station, up the steps until I was inside. There was an older woman at the desk I didn't recognize. Some new receptionist I imagined. "I need to see Garrett," I practically shouted at her.

"Now hold on there," she said. "Calm down..."

"No, I can't calm down. I need to see Garrett, now! Garrett!" I screamed his name and the next thing I saw was him sprinting out of his office.

He was here. I was safe.

"Brin, what is it?"

"He's here," I said grabbing onto his forearms as soon as he was close enough. "I saw him outside. He pointed at me. It was the same person from Dallas. I'm sure of it. He's wearing a black hoodie and sunglasses."

I didn't have to say anything after that. Garrett took off at run, barreling out of the station.

I stayed near the door, waiting for him. Logically, I knew Garrett was a law enforcement officer, but what if the stalker surprised him or shot at him? What if I had just sent Garrett into trouble? If something happened I didn't think I could live with myself.

That fear was quickly removed when Garrett walked back into the station. I didn't think. I just acted and threw myself into his arms.

I belong here. I always have.

"It's okay. You're all right," he said, patting my back.

"Did you see him?"

"No. Nobody fitting that description."

I sighed. "You're not going to believe me, then."

"Brin," he said. "Obviously you're scared."

I pulled away from him. All the commotion must have disturbed Romeo because he started crying again. I pulled him out of my bag and settled him on my chest to comfort him.

"What is that?"

"He's my kitten. I'm his momma now."

"You keep kittens in your purse?"

"I had to smuggle him into the Piggly Wiggly, okay?" Which I knew made no sense, but I was irritated enough by what had happened to not care. "And now I need to get him home so I can nurse him."

"You're going to nurse a kitten?"

I glared at him. "I have formula."

"Right. Can we step back?" Garrett asked. "Tell me exactly what happened."

"Why bother? You're not going to believe me anyway. I'm taking Romeo home. I'll make sure I'm not followed."

I settled Romeo back into the purse and started out of the station, but Garrett caught me around the arm. "Will you stop telling me what I will or won't believe when it comes to you? I'm walking you to your car. You're waiting for me to get my truck. Then I'm following you back to the house. Got it."

I had to swallow around a sudden lump in my throat. "You do believe me," I whispered.

"You saw something that scared you. That's all I need to know. Now let's go."

We walked to my car and I waited for Garrett to make it back to his truck before I pulled out. And if I looked at him in my rearview mirror every other second, just to make sure he was still there, I decided that was okay.

12

GARRETT

Pine's Ranch

I pulled in behind her Mercedes and followed her into the house. "I want details, Brin," I growled at her. I was still slightly pissed that she'd immediately assumed I wouldn't believe her about the stalker.

It meant she didn't trust me yet. Not fully. I couldn't have that. I couldn't have her not trusting me. I didn't think too long about why it was so important, I just knew it was true. Despite knowing I could never truly trust her because I didn't have that in me anymore.

"Not before I feed Romeo. I'm a mother now. He needs to be my first priority."

Was she kidding me? Her safety was less important than feeding a cat?

But I could see she was not about to be deterred. She assembled the bottle of formula with the tiny little nipple and coaxed the kitten's mouth open by rubbing gently under his chin.

Finally the cat got the idea after she plopped a few drops into his mouth. Then he latched on, and when she turned around to look at me the expression of wonder and pride in her face was unlike anything I had ever seen.

I nearly staggered, I was so thunderstruck by how that look made me feel. It was as if she had just discovered she had value in this world and I was discovering that with her.

I made my way to the couch and watched as she concentrated on her pet. As if she could will the animal to live.

"It's tiny, Brin. Really tiny," I said, trying to make sure she understood not to get too attached.

But she looked at me stubbornly. "I know. I know he's at risk. But he deserves a chance. His mother just left him in the barn and no one should be left by their mother."

I thought of her own mother. Barely present in her life. Only there when Brin had become attractive enough to deserve her attention. That was no kind of mother. And lord knew Hank hadn't been any kind of father.

It suddenly occurred to me just how on her own Brin had been growing up.

Romeo, simply too tired to eat anymore, fell asleep in Brin's hands. She looked at me anxiously and I thought I would do anything in the world to make her happy.

Which seemed like a bizarre thought to have, but it was there.

"Would you mind getting the supplies out of my car? I bought him his own bed."

Of course she had. And as I pulled the bags out I realized she'd bought about a hundred toys, too. It was then I had my second revelation of the day when it came to her.

Brin wanted to love something so bad it was exploding out of her.

What if she loved you?

Immediately I shook that thought away. I didn't want love. I'd had love—or thought I'd had love when all I'd had was a lie.

I remembered standing up in front of that church in front of all my friends and family waiting for Betty to walk down that aisle, thinking it was the happiest moment of my life. In those fifteen minutes I told myself she was just fussing with her dress or her hair. In those fifteen minutes I told myself she was having a battle with nerves. But somehow I knew. I knew in those fifteen minutes, before her father entered the church alone and handed me a letter, the expression on his face grim, that love was the biggest fucking lie of all time.

I wanted nothing to do with it. I just wished I could be honest enough with myself to say I wanted nothing to do with Brin.

I brought in all her stuff and watched as she settled Romeo into his bed. Some fuzzy toys pressed in with him to keep him warm.

"I'll need to wake him up every two hours or so to feed him. I should set a timer on my phone."

Yeah, like she was going to forget to feed the cat.

"Brin, enough," I said, catching her attention as she started to make her way back out the door to the car.

"Let me just get my stuff. I dumped it all out of my purse into my car."

"Brin." I grabbed her hand so she had to turn and face me. "We need to talk about this afternoon."

She tightened up but I pressed her on it. "I need details. You want me to find this guy right? Stop him? I need to know exactly what you saw."

She nibbled on the bottom of her lip, then finally nodded. "Let me just get my stuff and I'll tell you everything."

I relented and let her go. Then I poured us two Cokes over ice and set one on the counter for her. It wasn't diet. It was a full-on sugar, full-on calories. But I had this sudden compulsion to see her face when she drank it. To watch as the bubbles and the sugar hit her tongue and she lit up again.

Then I wanted to kiss her right after that. Taste the sugar that was the soda, the sugar that was all Brin.

It had been a mistake the other night to kiss her. To find out what I was missing. Because it only made me want more. More was a dangerous path once you started on it.

"Okay," she said as she breezed back in with her purse set to rights. "What's that?" she asked me as she stared at the soda.

"It's a Coke."

"A real one?"

"Do I look like the type to drink diet, Brin?"

She wiggled her nose. "You don't look like you drink a lot of Coke, either."

"I don't. It's treat. You know, every now and then just because it tastes good. Kind of like sex."

She blinked. I don't know why I said it. She told me the other night that she didn't care for sex. So she wouldn't see it as a treat, but I felt some kind of goddamn obligation to her to explain that not all sex was bad.

When done correctly it could be very, very good.

"Are you trying to bully me again?"

"Into sex?" I was doing it deliberately. Putting the word out there between us. "Don't be ridiculous. I would never bully you into something like that."

She cocked her head. "I meant the soda."

"Wouldn't do that, either. It's not a life or death situation here, Brin. I poured myself a soda and I poured you one, too. Drink it or don't."

I waited and watched as she reached for it and took a sip. She closed her eyes and tilted her head back as if she was feeling the pleasure course through her entire system. I wanted to watch her do that when I was pushing inside her with my cock. I wanted to see that exact expression, like I was rocking her entire world.

She put the glass down and pushed it away.

"Tastes just like I remembered," she said quietly. "It was really good. Thank you."

"Geezus, Brin, don't you ever just let yourself have?"

She looked at me, and suddenly it was like I was that glass of Coke. And she wanted to drink all of me down. My dick, which was already hard, throbbed. Thankfully I was standing behind the kitchen counter; she didn't have to see that.

"I thought you wanted to talk about what happened today," she said as a way to change the subject.

It felt like a bucket of ice-cold water being dumped over my head. Here I was thinking about my raging hard-on instead of doing my job. I was the sheriff. It was my duty to protect her as a citizen. Beyond that, I had made a promise to her.

"I do. Tell me exactly what you saw."

"I was coming out of the Piggly Wiggly and I just felt...like some one was there. Watching me. I turned around and saw him. I remembered the black hoodie from last time..."

"Are you sure it was the same hoodie? I mean, a hoodie is a hoodie. I need you to think. Did you see a face in Dallas?"

She shook her head.

"Did you see a face today?"

She shook her head. "But he pointed at me." She said it as if she was on the defensive.

"I'm not saying it wasn't the same person. I'm just trying to make sure, based on the facts, that it is. You're a famous person, Brin. Especially around these parts. A guy noticing you, pointing you out, it wouldn't be the strangest thing to happen."

"You think it was just some random fan? Then why was he staring at me? Why didn't he come over and introduce himself. Ask for a selfie? That's what fans do. Stalkers just watch."

"I don't know. I'm just saying that if the only two things tying the man in Dallas to the man you saw today is a black hoodie, that's not much to go on."

She slumped, but I knew she could see the reason in what I was saying.

"You think I might have panicked?"

"If you did, it wasn't for lack of reasons," I said. This person had been trying to scare her for months. That's what the phone calls were about. The dead cat on her door. The picture sent to her phone.

However, an actual confrontation is not something most stalkers did. They tended to stay in the shadows. That wasn't how Brin was describing these situations.

"I suppose that could be true," she said. "I just got this really creepy vibe."

"You're on a alert. As well you should be. I'm not saying we're still not going to take every precaution. And if I see a strange man walking around in a black hoodie you can be damn sure I'm going to have some questions for him. I just don't want you to feel as if you're not safe."

"I feel safe here," she said. And she said it so quickly it made me feel good. Like I had accomplished some feat.

"Good."

"I would like to burn off some energy, though. Between finding Romeo and...whatever that was today, I'm all jittery."

She wanted to burn off steam because she was jittery.

Don't go there. Don't go there!

"I was thinking of a run. Would that be okay? I mean, do you think it's safe enough to do that alone?"

"I'll go with you. Could use a run myself."

She beamed and I thought I would run a marathon for her if only she would continue to smile like that for me always.

Just for me.

SABRINA

I liked jogging with Garrett. He matched his pace to mine. Whether that was slower or faster than his normal pace I didn't know, but our strides were pretty even. We didn't talk at first, in the manner of true runners, we just got a feel for each other's rhythms. How our arms worked, how our breathing labored, until finally we were in sync.

And once we were in sync it felt...really good. I couldn't remember when I had felt this much in tune with another person's body next to mine.

"Was this really how you did it? You lost your baby fat by just running?" he asked as we ran straight down the long stretch of road between our two ranches.

"It wasn't baby fat. It was just fat. It's okay to say that Garrett."

"Not to me, it isn't. You act like you were some kind of freak. You were a few pounds overweight. I never understood the big deal, quite frankly."

It was more like thirty pounds, but he was trying to be sweet so I wasn't going to point that out. "The big deal was that I was Jennifer King's daughter. And not what she expected me to be."

"Fuck her expectations. What did *you* want to be?"

Since that question came perilously close to my own thoughts about what came next in my life, I really tried to think about the answer. The sad truth was that I didn't have one.

"I don't know. I didn't back then and I don't now. Which is part of my problem in trying to decide what comes next. You're going to think this is ridiculous, but aside from planning Ronnie's wedding, being stalked is the only other thing in my life right now. Which sounds really horrible when you say it out loud."

"What do you love to do?"

The word *shop* was on the tip of my tongue. It's exactly how the Cowboy Princess would have answered that question. Part of giving up the show, however, was letting go of the character. The stereotype that was me.

"I…well, I…I really love to bake." I did. I loved the precision of it. I loved the creativity of it. I loved the smell of it. I loved making other people happy with it. Seeing their faces light up when they bit into something I'd made was always special.

Like when Garrett ate one of my chocolate chip cookies.

"Perfect," Garrett said smiling at me. "Dusty Creek doesn't have a bakery."

I laughed, though at this pace it came out more like a pant. "Right. I'm going to open a bakery here."

His smile fell a little then. "Yeah, I suppose you don't want to live in Dusty Creek permanently. Probably used to the big cities."

"I don't mind Dusty Creek," I said, getting a little defensive. "I was raised here. Went to school here. I still have friends here."

"Then why not open a bakery here?"

"Because…" I stopped myself. "I mean, I guess there isn't a reason, but I don't know anything about running a business. Trust me when I tell you I don't think I inherited that gene from Hank."

"We're not talking about King Industries. You make stuff and you sell stuff. I'm pretty sure that's it."

I shook my head, not able to conceive that something as big as having a business could be that simple.

"I'll consider it," I said, more to appease him than for any other reason. Because I couldn't own a business. That was crazy. To distract myself from those thoughts I turned the questions to him. "What about you? Are you planning to stay in Dusty Creek forever?"

He puffed out some air. "Forever seems like a long time, but I have no plans to leave. I like the ranch. I like my job."

"Yes, but that ranch is more of a fam…" I stopped myself immediately but it wasn't fast enough.

He scowled, and if I wasn't mistaken he picked up the pace on our jog.

"Yeah, I know. But a family isn't going to happen for me. Ever."

It made me sad. Not because I wasn't going to be the person who had Garrett's babies. I had given up that dream a long time ago. It hurt that after all this time he was still brokenhearted.

"You must have really loved her," I said, trying to keep up with him but feeling myself getting winded.

That was when he stopped. Dead in his tracks.

I stopped, too, because I could feel a sense of anger in him and I didn't know if it was directed toward me or her. I knew I didn't like it.

"That's the fuck of it all, Brin. I don't know if I did or not. I thought I did, but how could I have loved someone who obviously didn't love me back? I don't feel anything for her anymore. I don't miss her. I don't even hate her. And if I loved her, if I really loved her...wouldn't I still at least think about her?"

I swallowed the words in my throat. Yes, I thought. If you really loved someone you would still think about him. There had never been a time I didn't think about Garrett. The first time I had sex he was there in my mind. The few other times after that, too. When things hurt me or made me sad, I thought of him. When things made me laugh and made me squeal with excitement, I thought of him.

I always thought of Garrett.

"If you didn't love her, then why can't you move on?"

He had his hands on his hips. He was taking longer breaths. He looked at me and suddenly there was this hunger in him. I imagined it was how I had looked at the glass of Coke he'd given me earlier. Sure, I wanted it, but I knew I couldn't have it because it wasn't good for me.

"We should go back," he said.

I nodded and followed him as he started running back toward his home.

13

GARRETT

Pine's Ranch

We were walking up my driveway, trying to cool off from the run. We hadn't talked much on the return trip and I knew that was mostly my fault. I could feel how surly I was. I wanted to kick something. Or hit something.

Or fuck someone.

Fuck.

Brin was so damn right. This ranch was a place for a family. It's what I had always wanted. Probably why I proposed to Betty as soon as I did. I didn't want to wait. I'd wanted my life, my family to start as quickly as possible.

Now I was looking at thirty in a few years and there was nothing after that. No kids, no Christmas mornings with presents from Santa, no woman waking up in bed with me, morning after morning, because I didn't trust that any of that could be real.

Fucking Betty destroyed all of that for me.

Because you let her.

It was true. I had let her, but I didn't know how to change that. Now I could hear Brin coming up behind me on the driveway. I slowed down and let her pass me so I could check out her ass in those tight black running shorts. She might have been thin, but what little body fat she did have hit all the right places.

Plus the sight of sweat rolling down her back was making me want to lick that salty trail. Taste her tanned skin. She was still panting a little as I came up behind her. I had this image of taking her hips in my hands and steering her to my bedroom, bending her over, pulling down her shorts, and fucking her hard and deep from behind.

I was hard just thinking about it, which was starting to become a regular thing in her presence.

"How is it possible you don't like sex?" I asked her—no, more like shouted at her. She had just gotten down two glasses from one of my cabinets and was filling them up with water for both us when she froze.

She turned off the faucet and handed me my glass. I drank the water in big gulps, watching her watch my Adam's apple bob up and down. When I was done I set the glass on the counter with a *thunk*.

"What?" she asked, taking sips of water from her own glass.

I came around the counter and moved into her space behind the sink. "You heard me. Why don't you like sex?"

"I told you," she muttered. "It kind of hurt and I didn't feel all that stuff you're supposed to feel like on TV and in the movies."

"Were you wet? With these other guys?" It was rude question and she was blushing now, but I couldn't stop myself. I wanted to see if I could get her pussy wet. I wanted to see if I could finger fuck her into an orgasm. I wanted to see how she would react when it was my cock plunging inside her.

"I... don't think we should talk about this. You said you didn't want to fuck me."

I laughed. "No, sweetheart, I said I wasn't *going* to fuck you.

Never said I didn't want to. But now I might be changing my mind."

Her gasp was almost erotic.

"I don't think you can do that."

"Why not? I need to fuck someone, and Brin, no one has ever needed a good fucking like you do. Especially if you've never come during sex. Aren't you curious what you're missing out on?" I was moving further into her space, and while she was stepping back she wasn't stopping my advance.

I could see the rise and fall of her chest. See that her pupils were getting dilated. She was thinking about it. She was thinking about me fucking her.

"I tried it," she whispered when I had her pressed up against the refrigerator.

"You never tried it with me," I said, even as I dropped my mouth onto hers.

It was as good as last time. She was sweet and hot and she opened right up for me. I wrapped my arms around her and brought her against my body. We were both dripping with sweat but I liked it. I liked that our fluids were merging.

I loved the feel of her tongue rubbing against mine. Like she was using me to explore what she liked.

I pulled her thigh up to my hip and pressed my erection against her center, and she moaned into my mouth.

Brin's problem with sex wasn't the intimacy. It wasn't that she was cold. Which made me think the guys she'd been with just hadn't done it for her. But not me. I had always done it for her, hadn't I?

It was wrong, maybe, to take advantage of those feelings she used to have for me, but I didn't care. I wanted her too much. I was about to start peeling off her bike shorts when the sound of a kitten mewling filled the whole downstairs, it was so loud.

Brin quickly had her hands up on my chest and was pushing me back.

"I have to feed Romeo!" she shouted. I looked at her eyes then, wide and a little wary. She had felt something and I thought she was a little afraid of it.

Good, I thought savagely. *Let her be a little afraid of how I make her feel.* If anything, it would only pique her curiosity.

"Okay," I said, backing off and giving her some space. Once free, she ran into the living room finding her cat still nestled in the little bed by the fireplace where she'd left him. She cuddled him to her chest like he was her protection. "You feed Romeo. I'm going to go take a shower and rub one out thinking about what it would be like to have you in there with me."

She gasped again and I loved it.

And, just like that, I had a secondary mission when it came to Sabrina King. Number one was still to protect her from any danger. But quickly following that I planned to sexually educate her on everything she'd been missing.

SABRINA

Later That Night

You never tried it with me.

I was pretty sure those words had ruined me forever. Because now I couldn't stop thinking about it. Sex. With Garrett Pine.

SEX. WITH GARRETT PINE!

I'd spent my entire teenage life wanting exactly that thing, and the last five years of my life trying to forget Garrett existed. Trying so hard that I'd had sex with other men just to prove to myself I was over him.

Even though I wasn't.

Tired of my thoughts, I got up. I checked on Romeo, cuddled in his cat bed in the corner of the room. He was still asleep after his last feeding. He'd probably had more food today than he'd had in his whole poor life. No wonder he was exhausted. Then I quietly opened the door to my room, making sure to walk softly so as not to wake up Garrett. Even though the master bedroom was at the other end of the hallway and it was doubtful he could hear me.

Did I want him to hear me?

No, of course I didn't.

I knew what he wanted, but fucking Garrett and then trying to put him in the past again would be too difficult. My gut assured me of that and he'd said very clearly he had no interest in anything else.

I made my way down the hall without bothering to turn on any lights. It was odd, but after just a few days here I felt like I already knew this ranch house intimately. Which wood planks on the floor creaked. Where all the plates and glasses were stored. What the stables smelled like.

Once I got to the kitchen I pulled down a glass from the cupboard and filled it with water. Instantly I felt cooler.

Except a light went on, illuminating the living room, and I gasped.

"Can't sleep either?" Garrett asked me. He was sitting on the couch in nothing but a pair of loose cotton pants, a beer bottle dangling between his fingers.

Which made me think of the loose sheer nightie I was wearing.

Which immediately made me think of sex, which I had already told myself was off the table.

Damn him!

"Come here, Brin. I won't bite."

Cautiously I made my way over and sat down where he was patting the place on the couch next to him. He put his arm around me, and it felt so good I nearly whimpered. I rested my head against his shoulder. My cheek touched his skin. I could smell him in a way I never had before and it was nearly intoxicating. It also made me feel so safe. Secure, like I had never been in my life.

"Tell me about your first time."

"Why?" It wasn't a conversation that would lead anywhere good.

"Because I've been sitting here all night kicking myself for being a cocky asshole with you today. Whatever experiences you had turned you off from sex, which means they couldn't have been good ones. I shouldn't have said those things. About being curious about what you're missing. Do you trust me?"

"Do you trust *me*?" I asked before I could think better of it. "Never mind. I know you don't."

"Brin..."

I shrugged. "Can you turn the light off?"

Garrett leaned over and did as I'd asked, plunging the living room back into darkness. It felt better this way. Less embarrassing.

"He was just some guy I met at a club," I started. "He asked for my number and called me the next day. He took me out to this really fancy restaurant and made a big deal of ordering all this really expensive food."

"None of which you ate."

"Not much of it, no. Then he drove me back to his place. When he pulled up to the sidewalk out front of his apartment building it dawned on me that he expected sex. It wasn't like he even asked, he just assumed..."

"Brin," Garrett whispered.

I didn't want his sympathy, though. "It was my decision. I knew that. I figured I was twenty, I might as well just do it. But it was more... I don't know...overwhelming than I thought it would be. He immediately put his mouth down there on me. I mean like *DOWN THERE*. And that freaked me out. Then he made me do it to him, and the whole time, I was, like, I don't want to do this, but

I did it anyway. Then he said…" I closed my eyes because it was really horrible to remember. "'I hope you fuck better than you give head.'"

"Prick."

"Yeah. He was. He did it fast, and it burned and hurt, and when he was done he called an Uber for me and said he would see me around. I cried the whole way home. Then, a year later, I was drunk at some party and this guy was hitting on me and I thought I would try it again. It still hurt, and I thought then that it was all overrated. It's like when people tell you they love kale. That kale is this super food and so good for you and it's delicious, too. It's not. It's kale. There is nothing delicious about kale!"

Garrett laughed. And then he squeezed my arm and brought me into him closer. "Are you ready?"

"Ready for what?"

He stood and reached out his hand to me. "Come on, Brin. I'm going to take you to bed and give you an orgasm. We won't have sex. This isn't about that. But I need to show you how good it can be."

I looked up at him feeling all the reasons in the world why I didn't think this was a good idea. But it was like I needed to know. I needed to feel what Garrett could do to me.

"Okay."

He took me to his room. "What about Romeo?" I asked, feeling nervous and uncertain. "I won't hear him if he cries."

Garrett immediately changed direction and took me back to my room—or, I should say, his old room. I was going to mess around in Garrett's bed. It was like I was acting out every teenage fantasy I had ever had.

Once we were in the room he pulled down the covers that were messed up from where I had spent hours tossing and turning.

"Do you want to be naked or do you want to leave the nightie on?"

"Nightie on!"

He laughed again. "Okay."

It was stupid. I knew I had a body that attracted men, but I don't know that I had ever lost the fat-girl insecurities I'd carried around with me for so long. He moved over and then tugged me down on the bed until were on our sides facing each other.

"Did you like it when I kissed you?" he whispered, and I could feel the warmth of his breath on my lips.

"Yes," I whispered back. I didn't know why were whispering but I liked it. The feeling of intimacy. Like we were two teenagers trying not to get caught by his parents who were just down the hall.

"Then that's all we're going to do for a while."

Then I didn't have to think at all. He was kissing me and thrusting this tongue into my mouth until instinctively I pushed against his body, seeking more. The hair on his chest, the strength of his arms as he wrapped them around me.

After what felt like an hour of kissing, which was unrealistic but it was longer than I had ever been kissed, I could feel his hands sliding up my nightgown in the back, then back down as his fingers dipped inside my panties until he was cupping my ass in his palms.

"I'm going to take these off. Okay? Just your panties."

I nodded. And he used both hands to slide them down my legs. Once they were gone, he spent more time just focusing on kissing parts of me. The inside of my ankle, my knee, then my thigh. None of it was scary or overwhelming. I spread my thighs and it felt like I was opening myself to him.

I heard him groan. Or was that me?

His lips and tongue and teeth high on the inside of my thigh were driving me insane.

"Garrett, I need more, I think."

And he gave me more, sliding his finger deep inside me. I was so slick it didn't even hurt.

"Feel that, Brin. Feel how wet you are?" He took his now-damp finger and ran it along the skin just below my belly button. I could feel the wetness but it didn't embarrass me like I'd thought it would. "That's how it has to be. You have to be drenched and so ready to explode. Then it will be okay when I do this."

I didn't know what to expect, but the feel of his tongue slipping through my folds was so different from last time. I was waxed bare, because everyone in Hollywood was waxed bare, so it was like every motion of his tongue against my skin sent shock waves through my whole body. Then he was running his tongue up and down like he couldn't get enough of me, until finally I could feel him pushing it inside me along with his finger. Or was it two fingers? I couldn't tell. I just felt the pressure and it was so good.

And then the flat of his tongue was there on my clit, doing this wave-like motion even as his fingers continued to thrust into me.

"Ahhh! Eeehhhh. Ohhhhh!"

I was screaming. Or keening. I couldn't have been quiet if my life had depended on it. And then it hit, this huge, giant wave of physical pleasure from my toes to the tips of my ears until I couldn't take it anymore and I was pressing my hand into his hair and tugging him away.

Immediately he lifted his head and smiled up at me. At least, I think he was smiling. I could see the white of his teeth. He pulled his body up along mine and I could feel his erection pressing through his cotton pants against my belly.

"Do you want me to..." I started to run my hands down his chest over his stomach.

"No," he said, rolling to the side and taking me with him. "This wasn't transactional, Brin. Sex between two people is about making each other feel good. And it's always about giving, or I think it should be. Did I make you feel good?"

I nodded against his chest.

"Then I feel good because I gave that to you. Do you understand?"

I thought I did. But I still wouldn't have been opposed to touching him. To stroking him in my palm.

Except he was getting out of the bed.

"Oh, you're leaving now."

He sucked in some breath. "I'm coming back. I don't want to leave you after making you come, baby, but I need to...I need to..."

"Rub one out?" I asked, thinking back to how he'd referred to it before.

"Let's say, relieve some pressure. Then I can hold you. Okay?"

"Okay." I liked the sound of that. Of being held. "Also, once you're done relieving your pressure, can you warm up some formula? I'm thinking Romeo will be getting hungry soon."

He sighed and I thought I heard him say that he was fucked.

But I didn't think about anything after that as I drifted off into a dreamy sleep.

14

SABRINA

The Next Morning

Garrett Pine was in my bed. Or, more accurately, I was in Garrett Pine's bed. A place I had dreamed of for years. I figured this was probably going to mess me up when whatever we were doing was over, so I decided to just live in the moment and memorize every detail.

The scruff of his jaw, the way his arm was thrown back over his head. The way he half snored. The smattering of dark hair all along his chest and down his stomach. I couldn't see beyond that because the sheet was covering him, but the sheet was...shall we say...looking for some relief from the pressure of what was beneath it.

I was still in my nightie. I had put my panties back on when I fed Romeo and it hadn't felt right to take them off again when I returned to bed. Like it would be too much of an invitation for Garrett to pleasure me.

And I didn't know why, but I had this feeling that whatever

path this took us down, messing around with each other, Garrett needed to be the one to lead. Not because he was the man, but because in many ways he was the reluctant party. Like he didn't really want to do this, but he either couldn't stop himself or was making the decision to put my needs first.

But inviting him to touch me was very different than wanting to touch him.

I did. I did want to touch him.

I glanced up at his face and saw that he was still asleep. I thought of what he'd said last night. This wasn't about a thank-you or a tit for tat. This was this feeling inside me that I wanted to give to him. Pleasure. Release.

I slid my hand under the sheet and rested it above his stomach. The snorting noises coming from his nose stopped and the sheet tented even further. I tugged it off his body and saw his erection pressing against his loose cotton pants.

It called to me. Without thinking too much about it, I slipped my hand inside the band on his pants and found him. He was heavy and warm and so ridiculously hard. I squirmed a little, rubbing my pussy against the bed and loving the tingles that shot through my body.

I thought back to when I'd first discovered what an orgasm was. The summer going into my freshman year. Playing out all the fantasies I had about Garrett now that we would be in the same school together. I used to hump the mattress for a bit while I thought of him in his football uniform, and that was all it took.

Funny. It was around the time that'd I forced myself to stop thinking about Garrett that I stopped making myself come. It was like the fantasy had been more fun than the physical release. Once the fantasy was gone, it didn't seem worth the work.

Now I was inching down the bed, my hand full of his thick cock, and I thought all it would take might be a few humps...but this was about giving to him, wasn't it?

I let go of his cock and got up on my knees next to him. I

didn't look at his face. I didn't want to know if he was awake or not. His body was awake and that was all that mattered.

I took his dick myin hand again and bent over him, just licking the crown. Like the rest of him it was warm and smelled like him. I licked it again and I thought how much I liked it. No pressure. No hand in my hair directing me where to go. Just me exploring his erection, pumping it in my hand until finally I took the crown entirely into my mouth.

That's when I knew he was awake.

"Fuck that feels good, Brin."

I lifted my head, but it was like trying to pull myself away from an ice-cream cone. Once you started licking it was hard to stop. "Does it? I only did it that one time and he said..."

"You ever mention that prick in front of me again and I'll get pissed. You're in my bed. That's my cock you're sucking. Talking about some other guy right now isn't cool."

I nodded. He was right. This should just be between us. I leaned over him again and continued in my exploration. Dipping my tongue into the tip where it was a little wet already. Salty warmth. Taking him then as deep as I could go, and then further because he was groaning like a man tortured.

Giving felt delicious. Giving felt empowering.

But it also made me feel needy. Like now I knew what it meant to have his girth inside my mouth, on my tongue, I *needed* him in my body.

I pulled away and looked at him then. His face was red and tight. "Garrett, I want to...can we...can you come inside me?"

His nostrils flared. His hand dipped under the pillow behind his head and he extracted a condom.

"Please tell me that's not from when this was your room."

"I brought it back when I got the cat formula, just in case this happened," he growled. He ripped it open with this teeth and, with one hand, slid it down his erection. "Come on up here and straddle me, babe."

I shimmied out of my panties first, then did what he asked. I wasn't really certain what to do next, but I didn't have to know. He kept me perched over him, my sex above his, my hands braced on his shoulders. Then he brought his hand to my pussy and started to slowly insert his finger. In and out. In and out. Until I started pressing down when he thrust up.

"Hmmmm. Ohhhhhh. Garrett! Please. This is good. This good. Good. Good."

He moved my hips then and positioned his cock at my wet opening, nudging the head of his cock inside me. There was that same sense of stretching, a little burning, but I realized the difference now that I was motivated to push through the discomfort. I wanted him *INSIDE* of me. If it hurt a little to get him there, then that was okay.

I shifted my knees so I had leverage and pushed down on him harder. Lifting away when it was too much and then pushing down hard again.

"Talk to me, Brin."

But I didn't want to talk. I just wanted to keep moving. "Unnnnhhh. Unnnnnhhh."

His hand on my ass, his other at my hip, guiding me, helped me to focus on getting there. Like I could thrash and flail about, but he had me under control. Steadily letting me use his cock until my nipples seemed to become these hard, tiny points. My whole body was shaking as I came.

"Garrett!" Fuck, had I been too loud? Was I screaming? I didn't know because I was too busy just feeling all of it. Suddenly I was flipped onto my back. Instinctively I wrapped my legs around his hips, forcing him to return to the place I wanted.

He used his hand to position himself again, and then slowly he was thrusting back inside me.

"Okay, baby. I think you felt pretty good fucking me. Now let's see how you like to get fucked. Talk to me. Tell me if this is good for you."

Talk? Form sentences? He was ridiculous. I slapped his shoulders instead, and arched my back and said the only thing that made sense.

"Please! Please! Please!"

He grunted and then moved faster, harder, and more deeply inside me than I'd imagined anybody could. Or that I would ever want. There was so much of him. In me. Around me. It was like I wasn't a single person anymore, but part of this larger moment.

"Garrett!" Another orgasm enveloped me, and my mouth was open and I had no idea what sounds were coming out because I didn't care. I just felt and it was so good.

"Fuck, fuck, fuck," he grunted even as he shoved hard with the three short thrusts. He groaned then and collapsed on me.

I turned my head and kissed his ear.

"Please don't forget me," I whispered.

GARRETT

Later That Morning

"It is incredible how I feel. Like I have no bones in my body. No wonder everyone brags about good sex."

Brin was sitting on the couch with Romeo cuddled to her chest as she fed him. It made me feel something in my chest that bothered me. I was actually rubbing a hand over the area that hurt and it bothered me again when I saw it was over my heart. I reached for the coffee cup in front of me and had the overwhelming sense that I needed to get out of there.

Brin's glow was blinding me, and while part of me wanted stand up on the roof of my home and shout to the world that I had been the one to bring her to orgasm, another part of me wanted to bolt.

"I need to head into the office," I said a little gruffly. "You're going to stay put today."

She nodded. "I have plenty of stuff to do to get ready for the engagement party."

"I thought you were planning the wedding."

"Yes," she beamed. "After the engagement party. But I can do everything I need to online or over the phone. Speaking of which, I need to call Ronnie and let her know my number changed. Again. Ugh. She's going to freak out when I tell her what's been going on."

"She's your sister. She should know what's happening."

Brin just rolled her eyes at me. "Bea is my sister, too, and she'll think I'm being dramatic. And Dylan's my brother and I doubt he would care at all."

"You ever talk to him?" I asked her. I couldn't fathom that. Having a family that was lost to me. When I used to think about having kids, I'd thought that part of being a parent was to make sure that my children understood that family was everything. After growing up an only child, I wanted to make sure my kids had more. Maybe even four or five kids. One big, massive, chaotic, loving mess.

Then I let all of that go.

The ache was back in my chest.

Brin shook her head. "The most we get is a text or maybe an email. That usually goes through Ronnie."

It made her sad. I could see it in her eyes. The next time I saw Dylan I was going to give him a piece of my mind. Hurting his sister, being absent from her life, was not cool.

Not that I would have any reason to see him. Once I found out who was terrorizing her and put an end to it, she would go back home.

To The King's Land. Where the Kings belonged.

"Well, have fun planning your party," I said in lieu of goodbye.

I should have just walked out. Kept things simple. Instead, I didn't move from where I was rooted.

Romeo, apparently having eaten his fill, had passed out. Gently she set him down on the cat bed she'd bought for him. She came up to me and I could see she was just as uncertain about what to do.

I had already laid (no pun intended) it out for her about what this was. I didn't do relationships. I didn't do long-term.

No, asshole. You fuck them and forget them. And you told her *that.*

She rocked on her toes. "So, 'bye, I guess."

"Stay on the ranch. No surprises. I'll do a drive-by at some point and be home around five."

"Okay."

Yeah, I definitely should have left then, but I didn't, and she didn't move either.

"I'll make dinner," she said, trying to fill the awkward silence. And it was me doing it. I was making things awkward because I wouldn't do what I said I was going to do and just leave.

"You don't have to."

"No, I insist. It's the least I can do. What do you like?"

What did I like? The sound of her screaming my name as she came. I liked that a whole fucking lot.

"Anything. I'm pretty easy."

"I can do easy. I don't cook as well as I bake. It's not as fun to me, but I'll see what you have in the pantry."

I didn't want to disappoint her but I doubted I had much in the pantry. "Just promise me no grocery-store trips if I don't have something you think you need. Make do with what's here. Got it?"

She pursed her lips. "You've told me, like, a thousand times to stay put. I've got it. Now you go off to work like the big bad sheriff you are while I stay here and futz around. I might even go muck the stables again. And I can't believe that's a sentence that came out of my mouth!"

She was smiling and glowing. Relaxed from a hard fuck and a few orgasms, and if I didn't leave that second I was going to have her again. And again and again until I purged myself of this ache in my chest.

"'Bye," I said curtly and turned before I kissed her. Because that's what I wanted to do. Not as any kind of foreplay. Not as a buildup to something better. I wanted the last thing I did before leaving for work to be planting a kiss on her smiling mouth.

Because I wanted it so much I couldn't let myself have it.

I walked out the front door, letting the storm door swing shut. I got in my truck, only to realize she was standing at the door waving at me. Like my leaving was a big deal.

She's high on good sex. It means nothing.

Except, as I started my truck and pulled out of the driveway, she stood there the whole time. I forced myself to look away from that, as well.

15

SABRINA

Pine's Ranch

"Ronnie, I know you're not picking up because it's a strange number, but it's Sabrina. Call me back on this number when you get a chance." I left the voice mail then hung up.

I checked on Romeo but he was still sleeping. Maybe it was my imagination, but after two days of constant feeding and a lot of love he looked stronger to me. My phone, still in my hand, buzzed and Ronnie's name appeared on the screen.

I took a deep breath and prepared myself for a dose of older sistering.

"Hey," I answered.

"Don't hey me. Why are you calling me on yet another new number? You just changed it a few weeks ago."

"Because I got hacked. Again."

There was a pause.

"Sabrina King, tell me right now what's going on."

"There is someone..." Another deep breath. "There is

someone stalking me. Targeting me. It started with emails. Then it escalated. It's part of the reason why I left LA. Why I went back to the ranch...although I think he's here in Dusty Creek."

"Holy shit! Sabrina. You need to pack your bags and come here now. Clayton will have a team of security lined up to protect you at all times."

It was funny. I hadn't considered it at the time, but Ronnie was right. Clatyon would do anything for Ronnie, and if Ronnie wanted me to be safe then he would make that happen.

"It's okay. I have protection."

"Who did you hire?"

That was a fair question. I hadn't really hired anyone. I probably should talk to Garrett about that. But talking about money after we'd had sex seemed icky. In fact, I was pretty sure that if I brought up the idea of paying him he would freak out on me.

"Um. Well it's more like he's doing me a favor. It's the sheriff."

I wasn't sure if Ronnie would pick up on...

"You mean Garrett Pine? You mean Garrett—whom you've had a crush on your entire life—Pine is your bodyguard?"

I winced. "Yes. I'm staying with him, actually. The stalker would know about The King's Land, but likely not about Garrett. So I'm safe until we find out who this person is."

"Sabrina." Ronnie sighed. "What are you doing?"

There it was. The doubt. The thought that I might be trying to pull some prank to get Garrett's attention. Having a sister kind of sucked when she basically knew everything about you, including all the dumb stuff you used to do as a kid.

"I'm not doing anything. There is a person out there who, I believe, wants to hurt me. Garrett is making sure that doesn't happen."

"And you're going to tell me that you no longer have any feelings for Garrett? That this is strictly professional?"

Well, let's see. Three orgasms. A lot of screaming and yelling.

Kisses that made me whimper…no. It was not strictly professional.

"I know what I'm doing."

She had the nerve to snort. "Sabrina, ysou know I'm only thinking about your best interest when I tell you, you should leave and come here. Bea once told me that everyone says his fiancée leaving him, literally on his wedding day, twisted him. Garrett's not the guy from high school you remember."

"I know that."

I fuck women. I fuck them and forget them.

Which was maybe why things had been so awkward this morning. For the first time he'd been stuck with a woman he'd had sex with. A woman he couldn't put out of his mind because I was essentially his part-time job.

"Do you? Because I don't want to see you get hurt. And the truth is, Garrett Pine has only ever hurt you."

Right. Except last night and this morning. And the orgasms. What was going to happen when he came home? Were we going to do it again and again? Or would he tell me it was a one-time thing that he wanted to put behind him?

This morning, after the sex, it had felt a lot like regret on his part. And he'd kept rubbing his chest.

"I know what I'm doing," I repeated firmly, because when you absolutely didn't know what you were doing, the only thing you could do was lie.

"Okay. Fine. I'll let it go. But can you tell me why I got a save-the-date card for my ENGAGEMENT PARTY?"

I smiled. "I told you I was throwing you one."

"And I told you I didn't want one. The wedding isn't that far off. Isn't that enough?"

"Who doesn't like a party? Besides, you can't back out now. I've invited a hundred of your closest friends and family, and Clayton's business associates. I even invited Bea."

"Sabrina!" It was her frustrated voice.

"Please, Ronnie. Let me do this. I've been going stir-crazy ever since this stalking madness started happening. It gives me something to do besides bake, and like I said, I think it will be good for you and Clayton to put all the old memories behind you and build new ones. Happy ones. Because you are happy, aren't you?"

She sighed. It was a happy sigh. "I'm ecstatic. If we're being technical."

Ecstatic. In love. Loved in return. I couldn't imagine what that would be like.

I fuck women. I fuck them and forget them.

"Fine. We'll be there."

"Wear a fabulous dress," I told her. "And I promise to be in a slightly less fabulous dress so I don't upstage you."

"Somehow I don't think that's possible. Okay, tell me if I need to do...anything."

I beamed. "Nope. You and Clayton just show up at The King's Land in two weeks and smile."

"I'm only doing this for you."

She was. I knew that. Because Ronnie was the one person on this earth I think actually cared about me.

"I know. And Ronnie...you know I love you, right?"

"I love you too, sis."

We hung up and I thought about what it would be like if Garrett also cared about me. There were times...no, I told myself. He was just being protective. And his having sex with me was probably more to prove how wrong I was about it than anything else. There was nothing I should expect from him, no matter how badly I wanted to expect something.

~

GARRETT

Dusty Creek

"Hey, Mary, I'm leaving a little early today," I told the station's admin.

"Sure thing, boss," she said without looking up at me.

No questions about why. Where I was going. Why I needed to cut out of work. It wasn't even like I had official hours. When I was out on a call or investigating a case, I might not even make it into town. But over the last year of having the top job I had established a pretty regular routine of staying and taking care of any paperwork until at least six.

But when I looked up at the clock in my office and saw it was only four-thirty I knew I wasn't going to make it. I wanted...I needed to go home.

I needed to prove to myself that this anxious feeling I'd had all day about leaving Brin behind meant nothing. I needed to show her—and me, too—that just because we'd had sex didn't mean anything had changed.

I needed to tell her that it was a one-time thing. And, despite it being the best sex either of us ever had, we wouldn't be doing it again.

I shouldn't tell her it was the best sex I'd ever had. She would read into that.

But it was. It was the way she just handed herself over to me. No restraint. No barriers. Hell, my ears were still ringing from how fucking loud she was. And it wasn't some show. She'd just been in the moment, loving what I was doing to her body.

Loving...

Shit. Yeah, I needed to go and do this now. Set things straight with her before they got out of hand.

I drove back out to the ranch way too fast, but since I was the law in this town it wasn't like anyone was going to stop me. I parked in my driveway and got out of my truck, and when I opened the door to my home I was hit with the smell of home cooking and chocolate.

I removed my utility belt and holster, set them on the table near the door, and slowly made my way to the kitchen. I saw the plate of brownies, the perfectly even, perfectly stacked confections on the kitchen island. Brin had her back to me while she was stirring something in a pan.

"Hey," she said. "I know you're thinking you want to eat a brownie. Which you should, because they are the best brownies ever. But you should save your appetite because dinner is going to be good."

I looked her up and down. She'd changed into a pair of dark skinny jeans, an off-the-shoulder T-shirt, and a pair of red stiletto pumps.

"You cook in high heels?"

She glanced over her shoulder at me and winked. "I do everything in high heels."

And suddenly they were gone. All the things I was going to say. Every line I had practiced in my truck getting here. The ache from this morning was back and I wanted to crush it.

I only knew one way to do that. I wrapped my arm around her waist, pulling her away from the stove. I turned off the heat under what looked like some type of casserole.

"But..." she protested.

"Come shower with me," I said as I pressed a kiss against her neck. Then I rubbed my face against that smooth, soft skin. The day's stubble would mark her, but I didn't care. Because when I was done fucking her I wanted to see all the marks I was going to leave on her body while I ate the damn brownies she'd made for me.

She tightened for a second. Probably had no idea what to expect from me, and since I was doing the exact opposite of what I had told myself I would do, I couldn't blame her.

But I was done thinking for now.

"Okay," she sighed.

Right. Because when it came to me, she was helpless. I took her hand and pulled her along with me to my bedroom.

"Get naked. Now."

I started working on the buttons of my uniform. I didn't want to have to wait until I was naked to undress her. Another hesitation, but then she was lifting her shirt over her head. Stepping out of the stilettos. My mouth nearly ran dry when she pushed her pants down her legs and stood in front of me in a black lace bra and matching thong.

"Did you wear this for me?" I had pulled my shirt and undershirt off but that was it. I moved toward her and cupped her lace-covered breasts in my hands. "Did you put this on this morning hoping I would walk in and do this?"

I dropped my mouth to her hard nipple and bit down gently through the lace.

"Garrett," she sighed.

"Tell me," I said, moving on to her other breast, the other hard nipple. "You did, didn't you? You wanted me to see you like this." I slid my hand down over her flat stomach and pushed my fingers into her panties. She was already soaking wet for me.

"No, I...didn't. It's just my underwear."

"Liar," I said, even as I pushed a finger deep inside her. Her head fell back and she groaned in that loud way she had, like she wasn't holding anything back.

I stepped away to give myself a minute. If I didn't take a breath I was going to throw her on the bed and take her hard. She wasn't ready for that yet. She needed to trust her partner. Needed to know completely that everything I was going to do to her was going to make her feel good. Until that point when she realized that a hard, mindless fuck sometimes felt better than anything.

I took off the rest of my clothes even as she removed her bra and panties. I took her hand and pulled her toward my bathroom. I had a day of work on me, and besides needing to wash that off, I wanted to take my time touching her. I stopped at the nightstand next to my bed and opened the top drawer to get a condom out.

"You know you don't need that. I mean, maybe you do. But I don't. I'm on the pill. After that last…well, I know I'm not supposed to talk about other guys while your dick is hard and all, but I was tested, so I'm clean."

The words ran through my brain.

You can come in her. You can come in her. You can COME. IN. HER.

"I'm tested every quarter. I'm also clean," I mumbled. I thought about what it would mean. What it might feel like. What it might make me feel like. I had never had unprotected sex. Not even with Betty. She always insisted I wear a rubber.

She always insisted you wear a rubber because she knew she was fucking some other guy.

I waited for the rage to wash over me. The sense of betrayal. I couldn't take Sabrina if I was in that kind of state. It wouldn't be fair to her. Except then she pressed her front against my back. I could feel those hard nipples pushing against my skin. And her cheek against my back.

"We don't have to if you don't want to. Maybe you think it's too intimate."

My silence was inserting doubt into her mind. She was worried about how I was reacting to her suggestion. That was good, I thought. It meant she didn't expect too much from me.

Because I didn't have anything to give. I was broken and couldn't be fixed. I had always known that.

I dropped the condom back into to the drawer and pulled her with me into the bathroom. I had a large shower stall. Big enough for four people to fit, if I'd been the type to indulge in that sort of thing. I wasn't. I preferred to focus my attention on one woman at a time.

The water quickly got hot and I pushed Brin in before me. She squealed as the water hit her, but it was more out of shock than any discomfort. My girl liked to make noise. I was okay with that.

I got the soap in my hands quickly and started to lather it, running my hands up and down her body.

"Now my turn," she said as she did the same. She was more careful with me. Careful to avoid my painfully hard dick. Just brushing her hands over my ass.

She's still so new to this. I'm going to have to teach her everything.

I dipped my head and took her mouth. She moaned even as her hands went around my neck. When I reached between her thighs I could feel the heat and slickness, and I thought about how that was going to feel on my cock.

Unable to wait any longer, I turned her and pushed her hands against the wall of the shower. Then pulled her hips back toward me.

"Spread your legs a little more, baby."

She did, and the sight of her braced, ready take my cock, nearly undid me.

"Is shower sex as good as other sex?" she asked.

I pushed my dick against her entrance and slid home. "You tell me," I grunted and proceeded to fuck her into oblivion.

"Ohhhh. Unnnnnhhhh. Ahhhhhh. Garrett!"

My ears were ringing again. She was slapping her hands against the shower wall even as the hot water cascaded down around us. The heat of her body, her slick pussy, were unlike anything I had ever felt.

So tight. So wet. I reached around her hip and my thumb found her clit. "You need to come for me. Now, Brin."

Because I wasn't going to last. My back was tight and my balls felt like they were in my gut.

"Yesssssssyessssssyesssss," she cried out.

She was squeezing me hard from the inside and my mind went blank. I thrust into her without restraint or control, and then I was coming, and the idea that I was pumping my cum deep into her body wrecked me.

I finally came down off the fucking high of my life, but I didn't leave her. I wanted to stay inside her, keeping my cum inside of her, too.

That's how it would be if we were trying to have a baby.

I forced myself to pull away then. She was breathing heavily, her hands still planted against the wall.

"Hold still. I'll clean you up." I took the washrag I hadn't used on her body and looked down between her legs. There it was. Starting to slide down her inner thigh. What was this? This feeling that had basically been with me all day. And there, seeing my cum drip out of her body I realized what it was.

It was fucking hope.

16

SABRINA

Pine's Ranch—One Week Later

"You have got to be shitting me."

"I'm not!" I said.

It was late at night and we were lying in Garrett's bed, naked, because that's how he liked things when I was in bed. It had been a day off for him. One of the first he'd had since we'd been together. I mean, since I started staying at this house. He'd taken me to Branson, which was the nearest town that had a big movie theater. We watched a movie, went and got some burgers. He made me eat a whole half and FRIES! I'd forgotten how delicious those little suckers were. And then he brought me home and made love to me.

He didn't even mind that I kept Romeo with us the whole day in my purse. Romeo didn't seem to mind at all. He just took his normal feedings and napped the whole time.

It had been the best day. It had been the best sex. Because

that just continued to get better and better. He showed me what he liked when giving him a blow job. I was becoming an expert in ball cupping. And he made me figure out what I liked best when he was giving me cunnilingus. Which, I agree, is not the sexiest word in the world, but he kept referring to it as eating me out and there was something about the food and sex reference that I didn't like, so I was sticking to cunnilingus.

"Say it again," he demanded.

"Louis Vuitton."

"Now the other one."

"Louboutin." I did this in my best French accent.

"You're saying the same damn thing," he insisted.

I laughed. "I'm not. There is a Louis Vuitton and a Christian Louboutin. People think they are the same when they hear it, but they are two totally different designers."

"I think I'll stick to Nike. Which pair of shoes is your favorite?"

I gasped and lifted my chin from where I was resting it against his chest so that I could glare at him. "You would ask me to choose between my shoes? Are you some kind of animal? I love them all equally, of course. Okay, don't tell the others, but my Choos...well there's just something special about them."

"I think I would like to fuck you in your shoes."

I snorted. "That would be a lot of fucking."

He ran his hand along my back and I snuggled deeper into him.

"I don't mind. You got somewhere else you need to be?"

No. I didn't. There was absolutely nowhere else I wanted to be. This past week with Garrett hadn't been like anything else I had ever experienced in my life and I didn't want it to end. There was just one problem. Theoretically, it did have to end.

There hadn't been an "event" this whole week. I went into town with Garrett on three different occasions and saw nothing.

Maybe whoever it had been had finally given up and moved on. Which technically meant I didn't need a bodyguard anymore.

I lifted myself up, but when I did Garrett's eyes fixed on my breasts. He was making his adoration of my body quite well known. I pulled a sheet around me to cover up so he could focus as I sat next to him.

"We should probably talk about that," I said. "I mean, it's been over a week since anything has happened. Maybe my stalker has finally moved on."

I watched his jaw tighten. "You're saying you want to go back to The King's Land, then? Tired of slumming it here?"

"Don't say that," I said, hurt that those words would come out of his mouth. "I love this place and you know it. I'm just...I mean, I don't know...I can't stay here indefinitely."

He sighed and rubbed a hand over his mouth. "I suppose not."

"Not if we're, if you're just...fucking around...with me."

He glared at me then and I waited for him to correct me. To tell me that what had been happening between us was more than just fun times and good sex. That it went way deeper, which was why he didn't want me to leave. I realized I was actually holding my breath.

"Right. I wouldn't want you to think..." His voice trailed off but I understood his meaning.

"Wouldn't want me to think we were serious or anything." I had a hard time saying the words, and I could feel my heart pounding against my chest.

"I told you I didn't do serious," he snapped.

I nodded. "I know. You did. It's okay. I'm going to go get a glass of water. Do you want some?"

"Brin," he growled. "Don't do this."

I had to get out of the bedroom before I started crying in front of him. Because that would only piss him off more. "I'm not doing anything but getting water."

I slid out of the bed and found his T-shirt as the first article of clothing that would cover me. I put it on and loved that it smelled like him.

"I'll get you a glass, too," I said with my back to him. I shut the door quietly behind me and made my way to the kitchen before I broke down and bent over, the hurt was so bad.

I told myself I could handle it. I told myself that I could just take what he offered and let it be what it was. I told myself I had kept enough barriers around my heart that when he did this, when he dumped me, it wouldn't hurt so bad.

I was wrong. I was so damn wrong.

I fought to hold my shit together, and in the end I was proud I didn't cry or sob. I just let myself feel the pain so I would know how it was going to feel when I did eventually leave. A smarter girl would have packed her things and gone immediately. Shown some pride. But I was never very smart when it came to Garrett Pine and I'd certainly never had any pride when it came to him, either.

So I filled up two glasses of water, put a smile on my face, and went back to bed with him. He didn't say anything when I walked into the room. I checked on Romeo. Garrett let me keep his cat bed on the bed with us so Romeo would know I was close. I gave him a little rub on his tiny head and then settled back in between the covers in the space Garrett had made for me.

No, I wasn't very smart. A smart girl wouldn't dig the hole any deeper than she already had. But it was like I couldn't stop myself.

"Goodnight, Garrett."

"Goodnight, Brin."

I thought about how nice that was. How I wanted to hear that from him every night for the rest of our lives.

Instead, I would take the next few days. If there were still no more threats or calls or sightings, I would leave. And break my own heart before he could do it for me.

~

GARRETT

Dusty Creek—The Next Day

I needed a drink. It was after five and I should have been heading home to check on Brin but I couldn't do it. I couldn't go back and face that smile. I knew it would be there.

She would beam at me when I walked through the door. She would have something cooking in the oven. She would have made some crazy-ass dessert.

But her smile...tonight it wouldn't be real. Not after last night. Not like it had been this whole past week.

After five years of one-night stands, suddenly there was this amazing, gorgeous, sexy woman in my home who made me feel like I was the best part of her day. And I couldn't go home to her.

I left the station and made my way to The Bar. I took a stool away from everyone else, sending the message I didn't necessarily want conversation.

"Sheriff, it's been awhile."

I acknowledged Jack with a chin tilt.

"Your regular?"

My regular was a draft of the house brew, but I felt like I needed something stronger than that.

I shook my head. "Make it a whiskey. Neat."

Jack let out a whistle. "Sounds like woman trouble."

"Is this the part where the wise bartender solves all my problems?" I snapped.

"I don't know. Do those problems have anything to do with Sabrina King?"

I glared at him while he poured my whiskey. "What do you know about me and Sabrina?"

"I know you've hung out here a few times. Had dinner. Sat at the bar. I've seen you around town doing errands with her, too. And, of course, there is the way she looks at you. Like you hung the moon or some shit."

I didn't want to know that. I didn't want to know how she looked at me. It's why I…I tried my hardest not look at her.

I took a sip of my drink and felt my tongue go numb.

"I know you don't look at her the same," Jack said, and it was like a knife in the gut.

Because he was right. I didn't. I wouldn't. I was broken. All that she offered wasn't mine to take, because I wasn't going down that road ever again. Fifteen fucking minutes. For fifteen minutes I had been the happiest schmuck on the planet, waiting for the woman I loved to pledge herself to me.

Who would put themselves through that again?

"You hear what she's doing?" Jack asked.

What the hell was she doing? As far as I knew she was planning a freaking engagement party and a wedding at the same time. If she wasn't in the middle of putting something together to eat when I got home, she was usually on her laptop. Any time I asked her what she was doing, she would say her job, which to her meant shopping for things.

"No," I snapped, pissed that he knew something that I didn't about Brin.

"Setting the vet up with an animal rescue shelter. Doc and Charlotte have been wanting to do it for a long time, just couldn't get enough donations. Sabrina King got her soon-to-be brother-in-law to pony up the whole nut. As long as it's maintained as a no-kill shelter."

"Yeah, that sounds like her." Like a woman who would bring her cat on a date and keep it in a towel-lined purse.

"Hot and kind. You don't find that too often, huh?"

I looked at Jack then. He was a good-looking guy. Right age. Someone Sabrina might date after we ended things. I might see them around town holding hands and shit. Because he was right.

Sabrina was hot and kind and a million other things. A good man would see that in her and want it for himself. Suddenly I had this urge to break his nose and make him not such a good-looking guy anymore.

"You didn't strike me as a poacher, Jack," I said calmly.

He laughed. "Oh, I don't poach. But I'm telling you this, man. If the situations were reversed, how long would you stay with someone who doesn't look at you like you look at them back? Me? Not too long, I would think."

I couldn't hear this anymore. I needed to get out of there. I shot back my drink and grimaced as the burn slid down my throat. I threw a ten-dollar bill on the bar and walked way.

As soon as I hit the street I saw him.

A tall, lean male wearing a black hoodie. He was heading for what appeared to be an old Nissan that looked like it had seen a lot of miles. I jogged up to him before he could get in the car.

"Hey! You! Stop."

He turned toward me. "Is there a problem, sheriff?"

"Do I know you?"

The kid put his hood down and I thought his face seemed familiar. "I'm Danny Wade, Pete Wade's son."

Right. I knew Pete had a son named Danny. "Haven't seen you around here for a while."

"I was working a well outside Houston. Dried up, so now I'm back until something else opens up."

What else did I know about Danny? Something about him and his father. "You living with your dad? Last I heard you two had a falling-out."

As I recalled, Pete had been furious enough with his son to kick him out of the house. He'd just never said what it was about.

"He's up in Wyoming until fall, working on a drill up there," he said, spitting on the ground while he did. "Only reason why I'm home. Me and Dad don't mesh well together."

"Let me ask you, do you know Sabrina King?"

He snorted. “Uh, yeah. Like, the whole country knows Sabrina King. *Cowboy Princess* and all that reality shit.”

“Yeah, but did you know her before that?” I pressed.

“She was a senior when I was a freshman in high school. So I knew of her, yeah. She was the most popular girl in school. I doubt she knew who I was. What’s with all the questions?”

“Just looking into some things for her. Have you seen her in town lately?”

He seemed to consider that. “Yeah, I saw her coming out of the Piggly Wiggly like...I don’t know, a week or so ago. I pointed at her and was like, oh, shit, it’s Sabrina King. Then it was weird because I remember she took off running. No clue what startled her, though.”

“You been to Dallas recently?”

He shook his head. “I told you I was working outside of Houston. Am I in some kind of trouble here? Because I didn’t do shit.”

I could tell he was getting defensive. Probably had every right since his only crime happened to be wearing a black hoodie and loosely fitting the description Brin had given me.

Of course it made sense now that it was probably Danny she had seen that day in the street. She’d just leaped to the wrong conclusion about who he was. Which meant there was no stalker in Dusty Creek.

Which meant there was no reason to keep her at my house any longer.

“No, you’re fine. See you around town.”

“Whatever, sheriff.”

He got in his car and I watched as he drove away. I had to go home. I had to tell Brin the man she’d seen had just been someone who recognized her and who had happened to be wearing a hoodie.

I stood rooted there on the sidewalk because I knew. I knew as soon as I did, that as soon as I told her she had nothing to fear anymore, I would lose her.

Because her smile, when she beamed at me, wasn't going to be real tonight.

17

SABRINA

Pine's Ranch

"Hey, you're running late tonight. Something happen today at work?"

See? That sounded pleasant. Easy. I smiled at him and thought there was no way he could tell I had spent part of the day crying over him. I told myself it was best to get it out of my system before he came home. I literally put it on my day's calendar. Two to three—crying jag. Three to four, ice and cucumber treatment to handle the swelling. Four to five, practice smiling and making chitchat in the mirror.

I watched Garrett take off his utility belt and set it down on the table in the foyer. If I'd been going to stay, I would get him a rack or something better to hold his belt and gun so it wasn't just out there on the table like that.

But I wasn't staying.

A few more days. A few more days with him and I would take every one of them.

"What in the hell is that?"

I flinched at his tone. He was glaring at the box on the kitchen counter like it was some kind of rabid beast. "Oh, check this out," I said, clapping my hands. I flipped open the lid. "Ta-da! It's a Kate Spade cat purse. See the ears and the eyes and whiskers on the front? I figured Romeo needed to be carried around in something more stylish, and besides, I needed my actual purse back."

I thought it was adorable but he was still glaring at it like it was going to bite him. "You ordered that," he bit out.

"Yes. From the website. Why are you behaving like this?"

"You had a fucking delivery person out here, Brin! Don't you get that? You have some guy who has hacked your phone and emails who supposedly wants to hurt you. And you order something and have it shipped here! Here, where you're supposed to be in hiding! What was whole damn point of you being here if you were going to let the world know?"

He was shouting and his face was a furious red. I couldn't think. I started to stutter and then I started to think about what he'd said.

"*Supposedly* wants to hurt me? When did we go back to *supposedly*?"

"Oh, no," he said, storming toward me. "You do not change the subject. How can I possibly think YOU think you're in danger if you're willing to tell everyone where you are?"

That wasn't fair. I wasn't doing that. But I realized now it was stupid of me to do it. The stalker had proven on many occasions he had access to my accounts over the Web. I had been careless and let my guard down.

"I...didn't...think...I guess... It was just a stupid purse... I didn't think."

"You didn't think or you know damn well this whole stalker thing has been a stunt from the beginning? I found your hoodie guy today. It's Pete Wade's son, Danny. You went to high school with him. He said he saw you and pointed at you because he realized who you were and then watched you take off running, but he didn't know why."

Stunt. He thought it was a stunt. I could actually feel myself shutting down. "Oh. That could have been it."

"Yeah," he snorted. "That could have been it."

I was shaking. I could feel my lips trembling, and I knew I was going to cry and I didn't want to do it front of him. I needed to leave but he wasn't done yelling at me, and I had this idea that it would be rude to walk out on a conversation.

"What did you think was going to happen here, Brin?" He waved his hand in the air. There was an ugly smirk on his face I had never seen before. "I bring you to my home. You make me some brownies and cookies. Give me some good and regular sex and I'm going to change and be the man you've always wanted me to be? Some guy that worshipped at your feet? That loved you? Because that was never going to happen and you knew that from the beginning! I. Am. Broken."

With his hand he slammed each word against his chest as he said it. I wanted to rub the pain away and tell him I was sorry he'd been hurt so badly. But I was pretty sure he didn't want to hear that from me. And I was done listening to his awfulness. The more he talked, the more he would ruin what this week had meant to me and I didn't want that. I wanted to the remember all the feelings right up until last night as being good and wonderful.

"Can I go now?" I asked.

"That's it? You're not going to say anything? Not going to at least try and convince me this wasn't all some kind of setup?"

I shook my head. "I just want to get Romeo. I'll come back for the rest of my stuff tomorrow while you're at work. There is a lasagna in the oven, so you should take that out when the timer rings."

I moved away from him while he stood there in the kitchen cursing to himself. I scooped up Romeo and his feeding supplies and then went to get my purse. My car keys were in the side pocket.

"Brin…wait."

I didn't stop moving. I had Romeo. I had his formula and nipples. I had my keys. I started toward the front door.

He stepped in front of me. "Brin…"

Then I felt it. A rage so clean, so powerful, I was surprised I didn't levitate, my body was shaking so hard. "My name is Sabrina King. You can call me Ms. King. Because that's all I am to you now, sheriff. Now get the fuck out of my way."

I didn't know what he'd been about to say, but it didn't matter. He must have realized that, too, because he did as I asked and stepped out of my path.

I drove back to the ranch. Made sure all the doors and windows were locked. Got my gun back out from the storage unit, took Romeo, and went to bed.

And I stayed there for three days until Ronnie came and got me.

~

GARRETT

The Bar—A Week Later

Jack walked to where I was sitting at the bar. This time I didn't have to ask; he just poured the whiskey and slid in front of me. I knocked it back in one shot and then pushed the glass in his direction again.

"You going to get drunk?"

"That's the plan," I said as I waited for him to pour the second glass. "But see that strapping young deputy sitting at the end of the bar? I'm paying him to drive me home. Out of my own pocket. Wouldn't want you to think I was abusing taxpayer dollars."

"Why is he sitting at the other end of the bar?" Jack asked as he pushed another drink in front of me. This time I just sipped it.

"Because I don't want company." That wasn't true. I ached for company. Just not my deputy's.

"If you were going to get shit drunk and brood, why didn't you just stay home?"

"Because she's there."

"Hmm. Thought I heard Sabrina was back at The King's Land. Her sisters and her sister's fiancé were in here this week," he said, explaining why he might have an idea of where she was.

God, just hearing her name hurt. Sabrina. What the fuck did I do? I took another swig of the whiskey. I had done the drink-at-home-to-oblivion thing most of the week. Working hungover had sucked. At least tomorrow I was off. But I hadn't been able to take being in my home another minute.

"It still smells like her," I admitted. "Fucking lasagna and brownies and the bed sheets... I've washed them twice but she's there. She's still fucking there."

"Hmm."

"What?"

Jack shook his head. "Just trying to figure out what's got you so upset when you dumped her."

"I didn't dump her," I growled. I'd yelled at her. Called her a liar. Pushed her away because she was getting to me. Making me want things I told myself I couldn't have.

That first night I'd spent angry at her for leaving and not fighting back. The second night I'd debated with myself if I should go get her back. That's when I decided to get drunk instead.

By the third night the doubt started to creep in. Maybe I could have Brin as mine. Maybe I could let myself be the man who worshipped at her feet...who loved her.

But on the heels of that was the memory of what I'd said to her.

I cringed now even thinking about it.

"Not what her sister said. Ronnie, is it? I asked her where Sabrina was. That I hadn't seen her around, and she said she was at home getting over being dumped by you. Have to say she seemed pretty pissed at you when she said it. You might want to avoid The King's Land for the foreseeable future. Especially tonight."

"What's tonight?"

"The big engagement party," Jack said. "That's why it's dead in here."

I looked around and it occurred to me that it was quiet. Not typical for a Friday night. I had completely forgot about the party. And then it occurred to me how stupid a party was.

It was like giving her stalker an open-ended invitation to come inside.

I had been driving by her house each night, back and forth, to make sure nobody was around. I had seen her sisters arrive. Clayton was Ronnie's fiancé, and knowing he and the other two women were in the house with Brin made me okay with staying away.

Because, while I didn't doubt Danny Wade's story, once I had calmed down I was reminded of all the other shit that had happened to her. Finding Brin in fear with a gun clutched in her hands hadn't been a stunt or dramatics. It had been real. All that crap I had shouted at her had just been that. Angry crap from a man clearly unable to deal with the fact that he was falling for a woman for the second time in his life and was shit scared about it.

Now she was going to be in a house filled with people, many of whom, assuming they were Ronnie and Clayton's friends, she wouldn't know. I couldn't have that. I'd told her I had her back, and even though she hadn't known it, I had still been watching out for her.

Why? I asked myself. Why? There was only one answer to that question.

"Shit."

"Kicking yourself for letting her go?" Jack asked me.

"I'm not letting her go," I said as I got off the stool. "She's mine. She always has been. I've just been too much of an idiot to realize it. And now she's gone ahead and put herself in danger and I can't have that."

Jack laughed. "You're going to crash the party?"

"That's the new plan. Deputy, you're off duty. Turns out I'm not getting drunk, after all."

He gave me a salute and I rushed out of the bar to my truck that was waiting outside.

I had no idea what I was going to say to win her back, but if I had to lock her in her room while she kicked and screamed at me, at least I would know she was safe.

Shit, she might even throw her shoes at me. Those pointy things would hurt. But it would still be worth it, as long as Brin was talking to me.

18

GARRETT

The King's Land

Geezus, there was a line to get into the party. Just like there had been that night five years ago. I vividly recalled Betty nearly coming out of her skin with excitement that she was actually going to see The King's Land and meet Sabrina, who had been on the covers of so many of those trashy gossip magazines.

The paparazzi loved the rich and the beautiful. And Sabrina was both.

But I remembered thinking how lucky I was to have someone like Betty. Cute, sweet. Someone who wasn't gorgeous and ridiculously sexy hot. Someone who wouldn't turn every man's head when she walked by.

Because Sabrina was that kind of beautiful on the outside.

What hadn't realized then was how beautiful she was on the inside. All I'd ever seen was the surface. Hell, that's all anyone ever saw of her. Whether she was on TV or not, because that's all she would let anyone see.

Except me.

Me, who she had trusted since she was a kid to protect her.

Me, who hurt her the worst.

When I got to the gate I was thankful they had at least hired security. Clayton would have thought of that, even without being aware of Sabrina's situation. As I pulled up, I was asked to show a copy of my invitation. Instead I showed my badge, which I always kept in my wallet.

"Has a problem been reported, sheriff?" the guard asked me.

I shook my head. "No. I'm actually a friend of the family. Just wanted to stop in and see if they needed anything. You okay with that?"

He nodded and let me through, which meant that, while there was security, it wasn't great. I pulled my truck up to where a person in an orange vest was directing traffic. It took another fifteen damn minutes to park. I was nearly out of my mind before I was jogging up the driveway to the steps of the grand mansion.

When I walked inside, people immediately turned their heads to look at me. I was ridiculously underdressed in jeans and a T-shit, but it's not like a man dressed up to get shit-faced.

The people here, though, glittered and sparkled. Just like last time.

"Oh, no. You're not doing this. You are NOT doing this. I've lived through one drama-filled engagement party and that was enough. I'm not doing this again."

I turned to the person who was barreling down on me. It was Bea. She was a shorter version of Ronnie and equally stunning. She was wearing some designer black dress and pointing her finger at me.

"You need to leave," she said.

"I need to find Brin. I have to talk to her."

"You've said enough to her. You wrecked her! And I'm not giving you the opportunity to do any more damage."

"You don't understand," I argued. "I was…I got.. I fucked up.

Okay? I majorly fucked up, but I can fix this. I have to fix this. But none of that matters now. You have a house filled with people she doesn't know and she's got a stalker who has been harassing her. I need to make sure someone has eyes on her all night and those eyes are going to be mine."

"Wait, a stalker? Is that why she keeps changing her phone number?"

"Yes. Who ever it is has been able to get into her email, hacked her phone. I can't taking any chances he might use this party as a an excuse to get close."

Bea bit her bottom lip. "Nobody tells me anything."

"I kind of got the impression you two didn't get along. Brin always said you didn't like her."

"Didn't like her...ish. But that's different when we're talking about someone hurting my family. Here's the deal. I'll find Ronnie and tell her we need to keep our eyes on Brin, but you need to leave. Seeing you is only going to upset her."

"Garrett Pine. You asshole!" I turned to see Ronnie coming at me from the ballroom. Clayton wrapped his arm around her waist and hauled her up against him before she could reach me.

I had the distinct feeling he'd protected me from getting my face slapped, not that I didn't deserve that. Or worse.

"Let's not assault the sheriff, shall we love? We promised this party was going to go smoothly."

Bea narrowed her eyes at her older sister. "Did you know Sabrina was being stalked by some creeper?"

"Yes, but she only just told me how serious it was. After she changed her number again I wanted an explanation."

"Nobody tells me anything," Bea repeated.

"Not for nothing, but it was reported on TMZ," I pointed out.

"Fan of tabloid TV, are you?" Bea asked. "Personally I never watch the stuff."

"Well, Bea, maybe if you called your sisters—*both* your sisters—more, that wouldn't be the case," Ronnie said in that way mothers do to elicit guilt. I knew, because I had a mother who didn't think I called enough.

"Can we focus on the real asshole here?" Bea asked. "That's him. The guy who has been breaking our sister's heart for, like, her entire life."

"Please," I urged them both. "I get it. You want to stake me to an anthill, and I will let you, but please let me just find Brin. I need see her to know she's all right."

Ronnie sighed. "She was in the ballroom last time I saw her."

I raced in that direction and tried to see through the throng of people. It wasn't like she would be hard to spot. She'd be the prettiest woman in the room.

"What's going on?" This came from an attractive blonde who was wearing a very conservative dress for a party like this.

"Madison," Ronnie said to the woman. "Have you seen Sabrina?"

"Sure," she said and took a sip of her champagne.

"Where?" I barked it loud enough that the woman flinched. Then she raised her eyebrows to suggest she wasn't the type of woman who liked to be barked at. "Please."

"She was over there talking to the drummer. Apparently they went to high school together."

I looked in the direction she was pointing, but didn't see anything. Then I raced up to where the band was set up. There was no drummer. It looked like they were getting ready to start again. I caught the attention of the lead singer and he came to the edge of the stage.

"What's going on? We're getting ready to start our second set."

"Where is your drummer?"

"Man, it was messed up. He had a tire blowout on his way here."

That didn't make any sense. "So you've been without a drummer this whole time?"

"No, this kid, Danny, ran into us in town and said he could fill in. We took a shot, but he obviously flaked. Probably just wanted to crash the fancy digs. It's cool. We can do this without a drummer."

Every hair on my neck stood on edge. Danny. Stood in for the drummer. Sabrina was talking to the drummer. Someone she'd gone to high school with...

It couldn't be a coincidence.

I started tearing through every room. I knew I was making a scene but I didn't care. If it was Danny Wade, if he had been the one stalking Sabrina this whole time, then his only purpose in getting into the party would be to get her and get her out. There was no way he would have been able to get her out through the front door without them being seen. It only made sense he would take her around back.

I made my way to the kitchen, which was filled with staff hustling and bustling as they loaded trays of food.

"Did anyone see a young man and a woman in here? She's tall, dark hair, gorgeous. He would have been thin. Young. About this height." I raised my hand to what was my shoulder. Danny hadn't been that big, and Brin was tall, but he still probably outweighed her by about fifty pounds.

One of the waiters nodded and I rushed to him. "What did you see?"

"Just that this guy was leading this hot chick out the back door. She looked wasted and she was kind of draped on him. He said she needed some air. I thought ,man, that guy is seriously lucky to have scored her..."

I didn't wait for any further information. I took off out the back door and looked around. I knew there was an access road that ran along the back of the property. A small narrow road, but wide enough to fit a car because, as Hank got older, he hadn't liked to check out his cattle operation on horseback.

My problem was how the hell would I know which direction he would take her?

"Did you find her?"

I whirled around. It was Clayton.

"He's got her. He would have taken off on the access road, but what direction?"

"North," Clayton said. "That access road leads by my old home. Then it reconnects with Route 10 at a crossroads. If he was trying to get to the highway to get out of town, that's the direction he would go."

I didn't hesitate. I made my way back through the house. Bea and Ronnie were both chasing me, asking me for answers, but I didn't have any time to waste. "I'll bring her back, I promise," I shouted over my shoulder.

Then I was out front and heading to my truck. I might have frightened the guy directing the parking because I put the truck in Drive and veered off around the property, bouncing among the ruts and rocks until finally I hit the access road.

I was driving so fast I might have missed it, but my headlights lit up a sparkling shoe lying the middle of the road. I didn't stop to pick it up, but at least now I knew I was headed in the right direction.

"Hold on, Brin. I'm coming."

~

SABRINA

I was woozy, but even as I woke up I knew I was in trouble. I couldn't see anything but I could hear the engine and feel the movement of the car. Trunk. I was in the trunk. Okay, that made sense. He would want me contained and out of sight. I had this hysterical thought—was that anyway to treat someone who had been prom queen?

Danny. I'd seen him at the party. He told me he was filling in for the drummer. Asked if I remembered him from high school. He handed me a glass of champagne and said I looked as if I needed it.

Which had probably been true, as the last thing I had been in the mood for was the party I'd planned. Summoning the strength and energy to smile all night just hadn't been something I was up for. My goal was to do the rounds and then make an early exit. It was Ronnie and Clayton's party, after all.

And they were so happy. So obviously in love. That, too, had been painful to watch, which made me an awful person, knowing how long it had taken both of them to get to that place.

I moved around in the trunk, realizing he'd probably spiked the champagne. I had only taken a few sips, but my head felt like it was filled with cotton balls.

Think, Brin. Clear your head and think. You're in the trunk of car being taken to some place by Danny.

Danny, who had written all those horrible emails. Danny, who had killed that cat. Danny, who had been in Dallas. This whole time it had been him.

He'd said he loved me. I remembered that. Right before I got so dizzy. But this wasn't love; this was a sickness.

I figured I had two choices. I could wait it out. See where he took me. Eventually he would have to stop for gas. Maybe if I continued to act like I was passed out I could take him by surprise.

Or I could get the hell away from him now. Eventually someone was going to realize I was missing. When that happened they would call Garrett.

God, just thinking his name hurt. But he would have to know what had happened. That if I was missing it was because I had finally been caught by my stalker. Or he would think I had run off as part of another stunt. That I was back in Hollywood, living it up.

I groaned. No one was coming to save me. I needed to do this myself. I could feel a draft on my feet. My one foot was actually bare. And I could see a patch of rust where there was a hole in the trunk. I could do that. Push my foot or hand out through that hole so anybody driving by would know someone was trapped in the trunk.

But I had no idea where we were. And it's not like this was Dallas. Out here you could drive for hours without seeing another car.

Think, Sabrina! Think.

What about the trunk latch? If the car was so old there was actually a hole, maybe it would be easy to pop. If the trunk was open Danny would have to stop the car. Then, at least, I would have a chance to run from him.

I was fast. But without shoes? I didn't know.

But maybe once I escaped he would freak out and just leave me. Or, if we were somewhere with other cars around, I could flag one down for help. Deciding it was my best option, I reached out, feeling the felt material of the trunk. I twisted around and kept searching until...there. That was the latch. With the only light coming from the hole in the trunk I couldn't really see what I was doing so just played with it with my fingers. Seeing if I could find some trigger or something that would open it.

There was a flat piece of metal tucked behind another. If I could just turn that. I could feel it give under my fingers and...POP.

The trunk flew open, and just as expected, Danny had to come to a stop. As soon as the car slowed I didn't hesitate. I hopped out of the trunk, took off my other shoe and started running as fast as I could.

"Help me!" I screamed, not having any sense of where we were. But as I was running I could see there was nothing around us. Just this narrow road and the flat Texas earth. I pushed myself harder and resisted every urge to turn around and see if he was following me, knowing that it would cost me time.

Only without shoes and running in this stupid dress, I could hear him catching up to me and then his arms were reaching for me. At least this time I could fight. I used the shoe I hadn't realized I still had clutched in my hand and tried to stab at his face with the heel.

"Fuck, Sabrina, stop. Don't do this! I love you! Aren't you listening to me? I LOVE YOU!"

I didn't listen to him. I wouldn't listen to him. I broke away and started running again, but this time he tackled me to the ground. He was trying to get on top of me and somehow I knew that if I let him, it would be over. He would rape me and I didn't think I could survive that.

I pushed at his face, and there was spit coming out of his mouth as he shouted at me to stop fighting him. But I didn't and I wouldn't. He was pushing his legs between mine. I heard the dress rip up the seam. I tried to scream again, but he covered my mouth and nose with his hand.

"Stop fighting me!"

I would soon if he didn't take his hand away because I couldn't breath now. I could see dark spots in front of my eyes.

And then, suddenly, his weight was being lifted from me. I didn't know if he was getting up to undo his pants. I only knew I could breath again. Immediately I scrambled away from him, thinking I could run again. And that's when I saw him.

Garrett.

He had grabbed Danny by his shirt. He turned him and I watched as Garrett raised his fist and brought it smashing down into Danny's face. Once, twice and again until Danny collapsed at his feet.

I don't know why. It was like I couldn't think straight about anything. But seeing Garrett there, knowing what almost happened, I started to run again. I ran hard and fast. I didn't even know what I was running from or where I was running to, I only knew I needed to run. Because that was the only way I could stop thinking and I didn't want to think about any of this.

But just like last time, I wasn't fast enough. Garrett had his arms around me and was picking me up. I struggled and fought him, too, but he was too damn strong.

"Sabrina, listen to me."

"No! I will never listen to you again. Put me down! I hate you! I hate you!"

"Sabrina! Stop it. Stop it now!"

It kind of sucked that I was such a pushover for this man, because when he raised his voice at me I was helpless to resist him. I stopped struggling, but he wouldn't put me down. Just held me against his chest with his arms. Like I was some toy doll of his.

"Now listen to me. I have to take Danny into town so I can book him properly. You are going to sit quietly in my truck while I do that. Then I will take you back to The King's Land and we will talk. Do you understand me?"

I understood he needed to arrest Danny. I understood I needed a ride back to the ranch.

"Where are we?" I asked. My voice was hoarse from shouting.

"We're on the access road behind your property."

"You can take me to the ranch, then. Drop me off first and then do whatever you need to do."

He hesitated and I knew it was because I'd made sense. "I need you to make a statement."

"That doesn't have to be tonight. I'm the victim of a crime. I assume there would be some consideration for that. Sheriff?"

I was right again. And that meant I would only have to spend the time it took for him to drive me back to the ranch with him. Which was already too long.

He set me on the ground, but only so he could pick me up again in his arms.

"Put me down," I said tightly.

"Not until I see what you did to your feet," he said back, just as tightly. He eased me into the passenger seat of his truck and lifted my foot. He sucked in some air through his teeth and I could feel from the wetness coating them that my soles must be bleeding.

He pulled off his T-shirt and I forced myself to look away. I didn't want to see his chest. I didn't want to be reminded of the week when I had been able to touch it and kiss it and snuggle up against it.

Gently he used it to clean the bottom of my feet, then he wrapped the shirt around my right foot, which must have been in the worst shape. Then he tucked me into the car, pulled the seatbelt across me, and buckled me in like I was some kind of child. Once the buckle was in place he lowered his head and took in a deep breath. I had this instinctive urge to run my fingers through his hair and tell him that it was going to be okay.

That I was okay.

But he wasn't mine to touch, so I didn't.

Then he picked his head up, as if he'd remembered a particular nasty task he had to do. Which I supposed he had. He put Danny, who was still groggy, into the bed of his truck. He must have had some rope or something in the bed of the truck because I watched through the rearview mirror as Garrett appeared to tie Danny's hands behind his back.

Then Garrett got into the truck, turned it around, and took me back home.

It was so freaking ironic that I let out this weird burst of laughter.

"What?"

I shook my head. "It's just so funny that Danny is the only man who ever said he loved me." I laughed again, but I could feel the tears behind them. I didn't want to cry in front of Garrett, so I bit the bottom of my palm instead.

After a while I could see he was working out what he wanted to say to me.

"Brin..."

"Stop." I cut him off. "I don't want to hear anything you have to say. And tonight, of all nights, you have to do as I ask. I thought I was going to be raped. You stopped that, so thank you. But that's all I have to say."

"Brin," he sighed. "I don't want you to thank me."

I didn't say anything because there was nothing to say. We finished the ride in silence. By the time we got to the ranch most of the cars were gone. The party was apparently over.

"I hope I didn't ruin the whole party," I said to myself.

Garrett glared at me then, as he pulled the truck to a stop. "Stay there," he snapped.

I knew he wanted to carry me into the house. My feet were throbbing enough that I also knew I had to let him. He opened my door and shifted his arms underneath me. Like I weighed nothing, he scooped me up against his naked chest.

It really wasn't fair that he did that. That I could feel him again. Smell him again.

The front door opened and Ronnie came running out of the house. "I thought I heard a truck. Sabrina, oh, my God, are you okay? What did he do to you?"

"I'm fine. My feet got messed up from running." I looked over and saw Clayton, Bea, and Madison waiting for Garrett to carry me inside.

Big, strong Clayton. "Clayton, can you carry me inside, please?"

I felt Garrett's arms tighten around me. "I can carry you."

"I would rather he did it," I said without looking at him.

"Brin, this isn't over."

"Yes, it is. You'll arrest Danny and it's all over."

Clayton walked up to us and reluctantly Garrett turned me

over to him. "I mean it, Brin. This isn't over. I'm dropping Danny off at the station and then I'll be back."

"You said I didn't have to give a statement tonight."

"I don't mean for your damn statement. We need to talk. About us."

"Okay, sure," I said.

He looked startled. As if he hadn't expected I would give in so quickly. But then he knew I was a sucker for him. Always had been.

He nodded. "Good. I'll be back."

Ronnie, Bea, and Madison flocked to me. Ronnie looked like she was torn between crying and yelling at me for getting into this mess in the first place. Clayton carried me to the couch and set me down.

"I'll go get you some tea," he said.

I nodded. My throat was parched.

"What can we do? What do you need?" Ronnie asked, kneeling down in front of me.

I thought about what Garrett had said. Thought about whatever it was he might want to say to me. He would be feeling guilty now that he knew the truth. That I hadn't been lying and that the threat from Danny had been real.

He would need all the evidence. I would have to send him the emails and then he would get mad all over again because he would realize that I would never write that kind of filth as part of some dramatic event. He would be mad at me for not showing them to him, but I hadn't wanted him to read all that stuff about me in that context.

Yes, he would feel guilty, and he would try to apologize, and it would hurt more than anything. Because the one thing he couldn't apologize for was not loving me.

That was just a fact.

I looked at Madison. "If you were to represent me, could I give you my statement? Then you could give it to Garrett, couldn't you?"

"It doesn't really work that way. If it were to go trial you would still have to be a witness..."

"That's fine. I just...I need to leave. Now. Before he comes back. If I tell you everything, will that be enough to press charges?"

"You don't have to press charges," Madison said. "He committed the crime of kidnapping. The county is going to press charges. So, yes, I guess as a witness you could give me your statement and I could present that to the sheriff's department."

I nodded and turned to Ronnie. "Then that's what I want. I want to leave. Now."

She sighed. "Honey, you've been through a terrible ordeal. We can make sure Garrett doesn't see you tonight..."

"No. Ever. I can't let him see me ever again. He'll feel guilty. And I don't want that and I'm not strong enough... You know that about me. You know I can't be strong enough to do the right thing when it comes to him. I have to go now!"

"I'll take her," Bea said. "Besides it's not the worst idea in the world. News got out fast when people realized what was happening. That you had been kidnapped. It's already made the evening news. Which means more reporters are probably on their way now. You spill your beans to Madison. I'll go pack you a bag. When that's done, we'll get in my car and I'll take you to Dallas. Ronnie and Clayton can deal with Garrett and any reporters who show up."

"You can stay in our penthouse," Clayton said as he walked back into the living room carrying a mug of tea. He pushed it into my hands and it was only then that I realized they were shaking.

I nodded and took a sip of tea. Then Madison went in search of a notepad and pencil. When she came back, she sat next to me on the couch and I told her everything.

19

GARRETT

The King's Land

I looked at the clock on my dashboard and cursed. It was a little after one in the morning. I felt like a schmuck because I knew by now she was probably sleeping, but this was too big to let sit overnight. Brin needed to know how I felt about her. Now. Before another minute went by. I hit the button on the security intercom and was surprised when someone immediately opened the gate. I drove my truck up the driveway and hopped out.

Clayton and Ronnie were waiting for me at the front door. I was prepared for this. Prepared to battle my way through, if I had to, but I figured I would try reason and logic first.

"I know she's had a rough night. I know you've probably got her tucked into bed. But I have to talk to her. I have to explain what I said. Why I said it. I was so...I was so freaking scared of what was happening that I..."

Ronnie held up her hand. "She's gone, Garrett."

I shook my head. "She said okay. When I said I would come back and we would talk, she said that was okay."

Ronnie shrugged. "I guess she lied. Look, Garrett, I see that you're upset but maybe this is for the best. You know Sabrina. She's worn her heart on her sleeve for years when it comes to you, and you've never really felt the same way. I don't know what happened between you that week she stayed with you, but if this is just about sex..."

I squatted down and grabbed my hair because I couldn't believe she was saying these things.

"Just about sex," I whispered. "You have no idea what she gave me. She gave me hope back."

Slowly I stood back up again. "You have to tell me where she is."

"I...geezus, Garrett. She told me what you said. You said you were never going to be the man to love her. What else does she need to know? That you feel bad for thinking she's been lying to you this entire time?"

"I was scared," I said, swallowing the lump in my throat. "So damn scared to want someone again. To love someone again. I've spent this last week kicking myself in the ass, trying to figure out how to fix this and being desperately afraid that I can't. But tonight I realized that I can't *not* try to fix this. I can't let her go. I love her."

"She's in Dallas," Clayton said. "At our condo. Give me your cell and I'll send you the address."

"Clayton!" Ronnie looked at him. "I don't know if that was the right thing to do."

"Ronnie, I spent five years in hell. Loving you, wanting you back, desperate to fix what I had screwed up. Garrett screwed up, too. You going to make him wait five years? You going to make Sabrina wait that long? You promise me you love her?" This he said to me.

It was easier to say now. Easier to let myself feel it. Because I wasn't scared anymore.

"I love her. And the best thing about my whole life has been that Sabrina King has loved me back. I just didn't know it until now."

Clayton nodded. "There is an extra key in the planter when you get off the elevator."

I rattled off my cell phone number as Clayton pulled his phone out. A second later I knew were Sabrina was. A second after that I was headed back to my ranch to take a quick shower and pack a bag, and then I was off to Dallas.

SABRINA

Dallas—The Next Morning

"You have got to be kidding. Are you bottle-feeding that cat?"

I looked up at Bea's horrified face and smiled. "Romeo is my baby. Why wouldn't I feed him?"

"I thought you didn't like animals."

"No, I just didn't like that hundred pound beast you call Thelma drooling over my Gucci shoes."

"I'm going to head to Starbucks. You want anything?"

"Yes! A triple shot venti latte with two and a half pumps of sugar-free hazelnut, soy milk, extra hot, no foam."

"You're getting black coffee."

I pouted. "You have to be nice to me. I was a kidnap victim and I have a broken heart. I can't do that on black coffee."

"Fine," Bea sighed. "Don't move."

"Don't plan on it."

I had Romeo and coffee was being delivered. I had all I needed. It had been late when we got back to the condo. Walking had been a bitch, but once we were inside Bea had cleaned my feet with antiseptic and wrapped them up. When she'd asked me what I wanted to do with Garrett's shirt, I told her to burn it. I knew if she put it in the trash I would just take it out of there and sleep with it under my pillow. So I could at least smell him.

God, I was so pathetic. I wasn't sure what actually happened to the shirt, which was probably a good thing. Now I was settled on the couch, feeding Romeo, and planning to spend all day doing absolutely nothing except feeling sorry for myself.

I heard the door open and shut.

"I knew you were going to forget it," I called out to Bea. "You need to write it down. Triple shot venti latte..."

My voice trailed off when Garrett walked into the living room.

"Brin, I said we were going to talk and I meant it."

I don't know what stunned me more. That he was standing here or that Ronnie had betrayed me. "She wouldn't have done that to me," I whispered. "She wouldn't have let you come here..."

"Technically it wasn't Ronnie, it was Clayton. And I think the reason he did it is because he knows what it's like to fuck up, and he knows how hard it is to come back from that. Especially with a King sister."

I pulled the tiny nipple out of Romeo's mouth and he yowled, but then he settled down and went to sleep on my chest.

"I don't have anything to say to you," I said.

"Well, I've got plenty I need to say to you." He sat on the couch, super careful not jostle me. "Brin, I fucked up. I was scared and I didn't like what I was feeling and how you were changing things in my head. So I yelled at you and said I couldn't be the man you wanted me to be when the truth was the opposite. I already was that man. The man who would worship at your feet. The man who loved you. Who loves you."

I shook my head. I couldn't let myself believe it. "You're here because you feel guilty."

His jaw tensed, like it did when he got angry. "I'm here

because when I come inside of you, do you know what I think about? What I have thought about every time I did it? That maybe you forgot to take your pill that day. Or that you weren't on any birth control at all. That I was filling you with myself so that we could make a baby together. That I could watch you get round with my son or daughter inside you. Every time.

"When Betty left, you know what I cared about? The humiliation. That was the number one thing I felt. Humiliated. Not crushed. Not devastated. But that humiliation...it broke me. I just knew I was never going to get over that. I certainly wasn't going to put myself out there again. Then you came back to town and I started breaking every rule I made for myself. You turned this thing back on inside me. I wanted you, and I wanted babies, and I wanted your damn love. I wanted that so freaking badly, I panicked."

"But why? You've always known I...had feelings for you." My heart was pounding and it was like I was struggling to breathe. This couldn't be real, right? This couldn't be Garrett Pine saying all these things to me.

"Because I thought if I let myself go down that road with you and you left me waiting at the altar..."

I cupped his face in my palm. "I would never do that to you."

He smiled and it felt so good under my hand. Like I could feel his happiness. "I know you wouldn't. Because you always put me first. But I thought if I let myself love you, if I took that risk again and the real me didn't live up to the fantasy me you've had in your head most of your life, I would be crushed. I would be devastated. And all that crazy fear just came spewing out. Just like it did that day five years ago when you told me the truth about Betty."

"You were mad then."

He nodded. "I was. You want to know why?"

"I know why."

"You don't. I wanted you, Brin. I walked into that high school office and saw you, and I thought, holy fuck that is the sexiest, most beautiful woman in the world. And then you smiled at me and everything about you came through that smile and I thought...shit. That's Sabrina King and I want her. I'm not allowed to do that because I'm engaged. So, yeah, you made me mad because you made me doubt myself."

I smiled then. I really had put a lot of work into my outfit for prom night!

"I'm sorry she did that to you."

"I'm not. I'm not sorry for one damn thing that has brought me to this moment. I love you, Brin. I'm going to fix what I broke and maybe someday you're going to feel a quarter for me the way I feel about you. In the meantime, we're going to start making babies so you can care for them as well as you do that cat."

Garrett's babies. With his green eyes and my sense of shoe fashion.

"Is this really happening?" I whispered. I was afraid if I was too loud I would wake myself from this dream I was in. I didn't want to wake up.

He leaned down, careful again not to disturb a sleeping Romeo, and kissed me. And it was like he said, the thing that had died in me the day I walked out of his house, suddenly it was back beating in my chest.

"Seriously," Bea squawked. "Are you kidding me? Garrett Pine you leave me no choice. Because my sister is obviously addicted to you and can't help herself. So I'm going to have to take a baseball bat to your thick skull."

I laughed as Bea stood there with two Starbucks cups in her hands and a look of murder on her face.

"It's okay," I said. "Turns out he loves me."

"I do. Even though I know for a fact I'm not good enough for you."

"We'll have to see about that," I said, and he kissed me again.

"Well I'm not hanging around here all day to watch you two

make dove eyes at each other. One cup is Sabrina's concoction, and the other cup is black. Have fun."

"I plan to," Garrett said, except he was giving me that look. That look that said he wanted to eat all of me.

"And watch her feet," Bea said.

"They'll be fine," he called out to her as she left. "No harm will come to them when they're draped over my shoulders."

"Garrett!"

"Let's go, future Mrs. Pine. I told my deputy he's in charge for the day. If I couldn't get you to listen to me, Plan B was to sex you into forgiving me. I've decided we'll do that anyway."

He took Romeo off my chest and settled him into his cat bed, and then he did exactly as he'd stated and gave me enough orgasms to make me forget the last week ever happened.

And my feet never touched the bed once.

~

SABRINA

The King's Land—The Next Day

"You know, I used to think I hated this place, but it's kind of growing on me," I said to Garrett as we approached The King's Land.

"Will you miss it very much?"

I looked over at Garrett. We had spent the day in Clayton's condo, but I'd received a direct order from Ronnie to return as soon as possible so I could update her on our relationship progress. Given the love bites I was gleefully sporting, it wasn't going to be too hard to figure out what we had been doing all day yesterday.

"Nope. Because you know what your place will have that this big old house doesn't? You. And that's all I need."

He growled under his breath. "Stop being sweet. I'm going to want you again and I swear, after the fuck fest we had yesterday I thought it would be at least three days before I could get hard again."

I giggled and then I reached into my Kate Spade cat purse to give Romeo a cuddle.

"You shouldn't talk like that in front of the baby."

Garrett parked and came around to pick me up. My feet were better, but if I walked on them I broke open the scrapes and they started bleeding again.

Once inside I called out. "Hey, everyone I'm home."

"Oh, thank goodness," Ronnie said, coming out of the ballroom into the living room. "I imagine they'll be descending upon us again now that you're back."

Garrett set me down on the couch. "Who will be descending?"

"Well, I'm sure you two were too busy yesterday...uh, making up...to notice. But the story of your kidnapping was reported the night of the party, and of course all day yesterday was about your rescue. They find out you're back here, they are going to want your story."

"Uh-oh," I said. "Reporters."

"Lots and lots of reporters," Ronnie said, agreeing with my assessment. She had her cell phone in her hand and set it down on an end table next to me."They are going to want an explanation of what happened. I've got Madison on speaker. Madison, can you hear us?"

"I'm here," Madison said over the phone. "Obviously, I've been following the reports on the news. Talk to me, Garrett. What was this guy's deal?"

"He said it was when Hank died," Garrett explained. "He'd been cyber stalking you since high school. You were this legend to him. Apparently he's got some beefed-up software to do that kind of thing. Then you showed up on TV and he started to get even more obsessed with you. His dad found out what he was doing and kicked him out of the house, but when Danny heard Hank was dead, he thought it meant you needed him now. With his dad working in Wyoming, he came back to Dusty Creek to... well, to propose to you. He was at the funeral. Then he followed you back to LA, then to Dallas, and finally back here."

"So, he really was crazy?" I asked.

Garrett nodded. "And very delusional when it came to you. He thought he was going to convince you to love him back."

I shrugged. "Wasn't going to happen. I've only ever loved you, and turns out I'm a one-man woman."

Garrett did that growling thing again and my toes curled.

"Uh, we've got bigger problems than the press." Madison said to the room. "Sabrina, I'm glad you're safe. Ronnie thought it would be a good idea for me to serve as your official spokesperson. I've been putting some remarks together. I hope that's okay."

"Awesome," I said. "I've spent enough time in front of the paparazzi. If I never have my picture taken again it will be too soon."

"What's a bigger problem than the press?" Ronnie asked.

"Uh...So..." Maddie stammered through the phone. "I just got word. It appears your brother has also seen the story about the kidnapping...and, well, he's decided to come home."

I blinked. "Did you just say what I think you said?"

"I can't believe it," Ronnie said, shaking her head. "You can't be serious."

"I'm always serious," Madison replied. "It's true. Dylan is coming home."

EPILOGUE

SABRINA

Dusty Creek—One Year Later

"Garrett what are you doing?"

"Come on. You know you want to."

I didn't want to do anything other than go home and take my pants off. I'm pretty sure they were cutting off circulation to my head. However, because I was such a sucker when it came to my husband, rather than protest even more, I let him lead me by the hand around to the other side of the bleachers.

It was a Friday night in the fall in Dusty Creek. That meant football. Garrett said he thought the sheriff should be there, which is why we went every Friday. I think he just liked watching high school football. And since I loved spending time with him, I tolerated it

"Watch your step," he said as we carefully made our way through the debris left over after the football game. Mainly hotdog wrappers and popcorn boxes.

"I might be able to do that if I could see my feet. Which I cannot because I'm so fat!"

He turned around and glared at me. "Are we going to have a discussion?"

Garrett didn't like it when I called myself fat. But there was no other word for the size of my belly. It had gotten so bad I hadn't even been able to wear heels tonight. Which was probably good since Garrett had picked tonight to take me behind the bleachers.

"Are you being serious?" I asked him.

"Tell me you didn't have fantasies about making out with me here."

"Of course I had fantasies about you making out with you under here! But you were too busy making out with Caroline. Who was not good enough for you, by the way."

He chuckled and brought us to a stop. The crowd was gone, the field now quiet.

"You're right. She wasn't good enough for me. You know who is?"

I put my arms around his neck and pressed as much of my body against him as I could, but I still felt a million miles away because of my massive belly.

"Me?"

"You," he said and kissed me.

"Even now when I'm soooo fat that I can't wear high heels."

He growled a little and put his hand on my stomach. "Stop calling my baby girl fat."

I rubbed my hand over my belly where said baby girl seemed to be comfortably resting for now. I'd had a hotdog during the game, and that might get her hopping all night, but it was worth it. Hotdogs were delicious. Besides, Garrett loved it when she moved around and he could feel it happening.

"I'm not calling her fat. I'm calling me fat. I didn't know it was possible for a person's body to get this big."

"Only one more month to go. You can do it, baby."

One more month where it was just me, Garrett, and Romeo. I was all sorts of scared about becoming a mother, not having had much of a role model in my own. But there was Ronnie to help show me the way. And Romeo was thriving so I couldn't be too bad at it.

Also, Garrett would always have my back. So, besides being an amazing father, which I knew he was going to be, I knew he would make sure I had what I needed to be a good mom. It was just one of the thousand reasons I loved him.

He nuzzled my neck and I giggled with a sense of giddy joy.

"Is this what you did with Caroline?" I couldn't help asking. Not that I was jealous. Garrett Pine was one hundred percent all mine.

"You should know. You were watching the whole time," he muttered.

What could I say? I was.

But that was then and this was now. Now I was the woman who got to kiss Garrett Pine under the bleachers.

Thank you for reading The Bodyguard. Hope you enjoyed it. Ready to find out what happens when Dylan comes home? Click here for his story now!

Turn the page to read Chapter One of The Bastard!

EXCERPT FROM THE BASTARD

THE KING FAMILY BOOK THREE

Chapter 1

DYLAN

When it rained in Brujas, Panama, it got harder to throw the drunks out. On a clear night I could toss a drunk man out of the Yaviza Bar and he'd sleep it off on the beach, listening to the water. But when it rained—thick sheets of rain, hot and heavy and nearly black—they'd fight me. They'd throw punches, or curse my mother, or—if truly shit-faced—cry. It wasn't a fun job on the best of days, but in the rain it truly sucked.

There was only one drunk I'd thrown out tonight: a man who made an ass of himself in here at least once a week. There weren't many others in the bar this evening, and it was relatively empty. I walked back to the bar, listening to the rain pounding on the roof, and took a seat on a stool. The bartender, a black-haired woman named Maqui, poured a shot of tequila and put it in front of me.

I wasn't the official bouncer at the Yaviza. That is, I wasn't on the payroll. But I was strong, I'd been in the military, and when I came here to drink I sometimes made myself useful. I got free drinks in return, along with the gratitude of the owner, the occasional offer from Maqui, and a room in the back to sleep it off on the nights I'd had too much. I could throw out the other drunks, but there was no one big enough—or dumb enough—to throw me.

I downed the shot and put the empty glass on the bar. I wasn't drunk yet, but I intended to get there. When it rained like this, the sound always kept me awake no matter where I went. The only way I'd sleep in this rain was if I drank myself into it.

What's your problem, King? Life is supposed to be perfect.

I looked around. The place was dim; with the excitement over, the remaining customers were nearly dozing off in their chairs in the steamy heat. Maqui took a rag to the bar in silence. There was nothing going on tonight. Nothing going on any night, if I was being honest. I'd left Special Ops five months ago, burned out and pushed beyond the limit of exhaustion. I didn't want to work another day, see another death. I'd packaged out, packed my single bag, and gotten on the first airplane that was taking off.

And I'd ended up here. It was supposed to be retirement in paradise, a carefree life, for once, that cost a few dollars a day. I was supposed to put my feet up, sleep with all of the local women, and drink. I'd thought I'd be relaxed for the first time in my life, finally, at age thirty-one after serving my country since I was a teenager.

I hadn't thought that I'd be...bored. Restless. Ready for something, anything, to happen.

That was the problem with living on the edge: it was hard to back away from it.

I signaled Maqui for another shot—she smiled at me, but I shook my head—and took the glass from her. The free drinks weren't really that big a deal to me, since the average drink in Brujas cost a dollar and you could eat dinner for less. The rent on my apartment cost a whopping ninety-six dollars a month, and that was for the unit that *didn't* have cockroaches. Not that it made a difference, since down here the cockroaches flew and banged against my windows. Another way to guarantee I'd never sleep.

I could always go back to the States. I could leave this hot, steamy jungle hole and take myself back to New York or San Francisco or LA, even Texas, to The King's Land ranch—my father's legacy.

Hank King had been a CEO and a real estate baron and a lot of other things, most of which made him obscenely rich. I was his son, but I was a bastard. My mother had been one of King's strings of mistresses. She'd thought she had a golden ticket when she got pregnant. Instead, Hank had dumped my mother, but he'd given me his last name on the birth certificate.

My mother had been bitter. When things didn't work out the way she wanted, she'd kept me from Hank and wouldn't give him visitation rights. Hank retaliated with lawyers; Mom retaliated by marrying a different rich man when I was two and hiring lawyers of her own. By the time I was a teenager, I was so sick of both of them and the never-ending war that was my home life, that I'd enlisted in the military and left the country.

I moved up the ranks to Special Ops. The work was hard and exhausting, and I'd felt like a shell of a human being by the end, but it kept me out of the States and away from the clutches of both my mother and my father.

Then my father had died. I hadn't gone to the funeral, hadn't answered any of his lawyer's emails about the will. I had told my sister Veronica that there was no way in hell I was coming home for the funeral. Then I'd deleted my Hotmail address, quit Spec-Ops, and come to Panama. It was dull, but no one here knew I was a King. They only knew I was American, I'd been military, I liked tequila, and I could throw a man out the door.

Works for me, I told myself. Or at least, I'd thought it would.

Sweat trickled down my temples and made my T-shirt stick to my back. I scrubbed a hand through my hair and watched as

Maqui reached up and turned on the boxy old television above the bar. Her shirt rode up as she turned the knob and one of the other guys at the bar whistled, but I looked at him and he stopped. Maqui and I weren't a steady thing, but I didn't let anyone hassle her. I knew she lived in a tiny place ten blocks away, where her mother looked after her four-year-old son while she worked. I knew she sometimes liked a no-strings fuck just like I did, and that her life was too complicated for more. Assholes at the bar were the last thing she needed.

The TV blared to life. A baseball game came on, the announcers speaking in Spanish. Maqui clicked the antique remote control and the image flipped to a soap opera, a woman weeping with smeared mascara as she shouted at a man who was leaving and slamming the door. Maqui rolled her eyes and clicked the remote again.

"*—kidnapping of heiress Sabrina King—*"

Maqui hit the button and the image flipped to two puppets dancing on the screen, singing in Spanish.

"Maqui," I said, my voice sharper than I intended. "Go back."

She looked at me, blinking her long dark lashes. I'd spoken in English, which I didn't usually do with her. Her English wasn't great, but it was good enough, and she caught my drift. She hit the button.

"*—not clear if ransom is a motive. What we do know is that the high-profile reality star was taken from her home during an engagement party thrown for her sister—*"

"Hey!" one of the men across the bar shouted in Spanish. "Put the baseball game back on again! I don't want to see this shit!"

I barely heard him. I was leaning back on my stool, my attention glued to the crappy TV screen. A female newscaster was speaking in front of a photograph of a gorgeous young woman, her dark hair cascading around her shoulders, her makeup perfect, pink gloss on her smiling lips. She seemed to be wearing a dress made of a few knots of material and not much else. She looked like a spoiled socialite, but she didn't have a socialite's blank, polite expression. Instead, she looked like the kind of girl who could tell you a rude joke and cuss you out. The picture had caught her on the edge of a laugh, as if the photographer had said something funny.

I knew that face. I knew that laugh.

Jesus. Sabrina King. My half sister.

I had three half sisters. Ronnie and Bea were from one of Hank's wives. Sabrina was from yet another mistress, one he'd married after Ronnie and Bea's mother died. Hank had been a real class act, and he didn't always use protection.

"*—disappeared from her sister's engagement party at the Texas ranch that had belonged to her late father, real estate tycoon Hank King. There were reports last month that Sabrina King ended her reality show,* Cowboy Princess, *and left Los Angeles due to threats from a stalker.*"

Someone had taken Sabrina. My littlest half sister, the one who had been sweet and overweight as a kid, then had grown into a sexy, gorgeous TV star. The half sister my military brothers teased me about relentlessly. *Hell, that's your sister? Hot damn. Can you get me her number or what?*

But we weren't close. I'd been shit to my sisters, and it wasn't their fault. Ronnie was the dutiful one, sending me updates and big news when it happened, even though my replies were always one sentence, usually sent from an ancient laptop in a barracks in a godforsaken desert somewhere while the Wi-Fi cut in and out and the guy behind me told me to hurry the fuck up. Bea was trouble, and she wasn't interested in me, so I never heard from her at all. But Sabrina was the sister who could have maybe used a big brother. A real one.

"Hey!" the man shouted again. "Turn the channel!"

"Yeah," his companion added, also in Spanish. "No one cares about this stupid American TV star. Put the baseball back on!"

I glanced at Maqui. She was watching me, her expression

unreadable. *Someone took Sabrina.* I was seeing red, and my entire world was fucking rocked—but none of these people knew it because they didn't know who I was.

Don't let on, idiot. Keep it together. I nodded at Maqui, a little stiffly maybe. "It's okay," I said, in English again. "Change the channel."

She frowned and turned back to the TV. She switched back to the baseball game, and the other men at the bar muttered happily, then began commenting on the game. No one paid any attention to me, which was what I wanted. I pushed my stool back and stood.

Maqui glanced at me. "Another?" she asked.

I shook my head. My urge to get drunk was gone. Sabrina had been abducted straight from the goddamned ranch, where she should have been secure. Where the hell was her security detail? What about the cameras and the electronic alarms? Had she taken any personal belongings? Had they seen anyone strange hanging around the ranch lately?

The questions tumbled through my mind, each on the heels of the other. Because I'd had a specialty in Special Ops: kidnappings. The high-profile ones that came with ransom demands. I was skilled in getting people out of those situations—without bloodshed, if possible, but if it wasn't possible—well, I had training and skills, and I knew how to use them.

Skills I could use to find Sabrina right now, if I was in the middle of the action instead of sitting in this hellhole.

I had to get out of here, now.

I'd been here for months, but it would take me fifteen minutes at most to clear out. Pack my single bag, leave a note in Spanish for my landlord along with a few dollars. There was no one here to even say goodbye to.

It was seven hours' drive to the nearest airport, over roads that were sketchy at best. The rain wouldn't help. Still, I'd get there as fast as I could. If I wasn't already too late and Sabrina wasn't already dead.

If I wanted excitement, it looked like I was about to get it.

I turned to the door and glanced at Maqui one last time, to say something—what, I had no idea. Not goodbye, because we'd never been anything to each other in the first place except a few casual fucks. We had always been clear on that. But she was still watching me, and her expression had gone stony.

"She is very pretty, yes?" she said to me in English.

Sabrina. She was talking about Sabrina. "It isn't what you think," I said.

Maqui shrugged, her expression still hard. Whether she followed what I'd said, or simply didn't care, I couldn't tell. "You know this pretty girl, Sabrina King," she said. "You're leaving for her."

The men who came to the Yaviza Bar liked to make passes at Maqui. They all wanted to get into her bed. I was the only man she'd said yes to—in fact, it had been her idea. She had made me an offer one night, and I hadn't said no. It was an offer she hadn't made anyone else since her child's father left.

If she was attached, then that was too bad, because whatever we had was done. But she had the wrong idea about why.

I hesitated, the words on the tip of my tongue: *she's my sister.* But the King family was too famous, too prominent, and far too rich. It would be all over town in seconds. I couldn't admit to her that I was one of them. The instinct, even after all these years, was always to protect the family. The name. The privacy. At any cost.

So I settled for an explanation that wasn't one. "She isn't mine."

Maqui picked up a glass from the bar and turned away. "Goodbye, Dylan."

Well, I fucked that up. I should have played it differently, somehow, though I was damned if I could see how. In the meantime, someone could be hurting Sabrina with every second that passed. I turned and walked out the door.

It was time to go home after all these years. Time to be useful for the first time in forever. Time to be, however reluctantly, a King.

I was going back. And there was nothing anyone could do to stop me.

ALSO BY S. DOYLE

The Bride

The Wife

The Lover

The Baby

The Homecoming

The Bad Assassin

Catching The Billionaire

Dating The Superhero

My Crazy Ex-Superhero

Keep up with my latest news and releases by signing up for my newsletter!

http://bit.ly/SDoylenewsletter

Made in United States
Orlando, FL
05 November 2021